# The Man in the
# Gray Duster

# The Man in the Gray Duster

Carol Montgomery Mysteries #4

Fenton R. Kay

BORDERLANDS MEDIA

# Table of Contents

# Chapter One

It was cold, and the sun was rising. The first supply train of the year headed to Santa Fe had arrived at the crossroads — Las Cruces — on the Camino Real de la Tierra Adentro – the Camino — and was getting ready to continue north. It had been a hard winter in the tiny town of Las Cruces.

Now, the couple was putting their firstborn in the ground. The winter had stolen their precious jewel. The mother's eyes were puffy, but there were no more tears. Ashes to ashes, dust to dust – they weren't supposed to be there. The child would not even have a proper burial. Into the ground, a mumbled prayer, then they would be gone – again.

The man in the gray duster and hat shoveled the last bit of dirt into the hole. The tiny, white-wrapped bundle was gone – forever. The man and the woman climbed into the wagon; the man adjusted the duster under him, flicked the reins, and the horse walked north.

It started to snow. A skilled man could find work and a place to live in the north, in Santa Fe — so he had been told. He had tried, in the south, in Las Cruces. He had built a small adobe and was getting jobs in the town, then someone had purchased the land. Now, he and his wife were on the road again.

Amilee Lopez picked up the phone on her desk, "Good morning. Camponotus Renovation. This is Mrs. Lopez. How may I help you? ...Yes, sir. Doctor Montgomery is still out of town. We expect her back next week. ...Yes, sir, we are familiar with that house. I will send her an email and let her know of your interest. Thank you, sir. Can you give me your full name and email, please? Doctor Montgomery will probably email you back. That's George Percival? Email is 'Flummoxed@gmail.com'. Got it. Thank you."

Amilee hung up the office phone, picked up her cell phone, and opened up her emails.

> *Carol, you got a call from George Percival. Funny name for a guy with a Near-Eastern accent. He's the new owner of the property at Hadley and Espina. The one with the sinking corner. He wants to discuss a contract to re-engineer that corner. His email is Flummoxed@gmail.com. I told him you would email him and that you were due back in town next week.*
>
> *- Ami*

Ami clicked her phone off and leaned back in her chair. She sat forward again, looked at her watch, mumbled about supper, got up, locked the office door, and left. Not long after, she pulled into her driveway next to her son's car. *Hmm – Iggy's not home yet, but Anthony's here. I wonder what's up?*

"Mom, Dad's not home yet, and we have a leak under our sink. Can I borrow some tools and fix-it stuff?" He greeted her with a hug.

"Yes, for sure, mijo. Your dad's in Alamo - said he would probably be late for supper. How's my nieta and her mom?"

Over his shoulder, as he headed out the back door, "LeeAnn is fine and growing like a weed – still needing a boob in the middle of the night. Trish is struggling with that online class of hers. Trish's mom is watching LeeAnn for her. I'm fighting with my thesis committee – SNAFU – situation normal – 'all fouled up', as Dad would say. The tools are in the shop, yes?"

"Yep, wrenches should be hanging from the wall behind the bench. Tape in the drawer of the toolbox. Don't forget where you borrowed them. Give Trish a hug for me and tickle my round-cheeked granddaughter. Say hi to Trish's mom. Drive careful, mijo. Love you."

"Thanks, mom. See you guys tomorrow, yes? Oh, yeah - when's Carol due back?"

"Her last email said Sunday, barring weather-related lashups."

"Okay, bye. Love you, too."

Ami watched her son through the kitchen window as he entered the shop. Amazing how fast they grow up. *Shit, I'm too young to be a grandmother. But, hey, what a cutie – she looks just like her other grandmother. Okay, supper.*

⌂ ⌂ ⌂

Carol Montgomery and her husband, Lyle Parnassus, walked out of the loading ramp and into the El Paso airport waiting area. Rogue, in Carol's carrying case, meowed piteously. Carol took a deep breath and then started walking toward the terminal.

"Gads, Carol – it is nice to be home, even if home is still an hour away," Lyle said as he walked beside Carol.

*Boss, I need out of here. Can't you hurry?*

**Not yet, your meowness. We still have to get out to the long-term parking lot.**

*My bladder's about to pop.*

**Rogue, I'm going as fast as I can.**

"Agreed, my love. We'd better hurry, though. Rogue needs to find a sandbox.

*Hmpf – you dawdle along while your poor, long-suffering familiar dies an ugly death from pee poisoning.*

**Pobrecita, you'll survive. Now let me concentrate on negotiating this crowd, or we never will get outside.**

"Rogue has a problem, I take it," Lyle said to Carol as she barely avoided bumping into another walker.

"Yes – full bladderitis. I wonder if there's a dirt spot somewhere near or in the long-term lot?

*There had better be, or you will have a wet, stinky familiar and a wet, stinky cat carrier.*

# Chapter Two

A uniformed TSA officer stood in the corridor, watching people as they passed. "Excuse me, are you Drs. Montgomery and Parnassus?" the officer asked as Carol and Lyle approached.

"Yes, I'm Dr. Montgomery; why do you ask?"

"Would you follow me, please? I have been asked to bring you to the security office."

"Okay, but my cat, Rogue, has a full bladder."

Rogue meowed piteously.

"We've been on planes for nearly twenty-four hours since we left Marrakech. I couldn't get her to use the airplane toilets. Can we see if she can use a people potty in that ladies' room?" Carol replied, pointing toward a door on their right.

*Yes, yes, yes – hurry.*

"Hmm – I guess, let me check with my boss," and the officer spoke into her shoulder microphone. "Hello – Officer Cruz, here.

I'm with Doctors Montgomery and Parnassus, per directions. Dr. Montgomery is requesting a stop in the ladies' room. Is that okay?"

"Yes, but keep an eye on the cat carrier," the voice on the radio replied.

"You heard that, Dr. Montgomery, yes?"

"Yes, I did. Why the special concern about the cat carrier?"

"I don't know, ma'am. That information is above my pay rate," the Officer replied, smiling.

"OK, let's see if my cat will use the potty."

***You heard all that, Rogue. Can you use a people potty?***

*Yes, but soonest, please.*

Carol smiled and turned, followed by the TSA officer, toward the ladies' room. Inside, Carol opened the carrier, and Rogue jumped onto the toilet seat, hanging her rear end over the rim. The officer took the cat carrier and set it on a baby-changing shelf. Rogue peed in the toilet, then jumped onto the shelf and back into the carrier.

*Whew, not a moment too soon. I wonder what's going on?*

***We'll find out soon enough. Be patient.***

*Hmm – but why my carrier?*

***As I said, be patient – all will be revealed.***

Carol closed the carrier, and she and the officer exited the ladies' room. As they left, several women entered and gave them quizzical looks. Carol simply smiled. Lyle had been standing outside the door, waiting.

"Okay, Officer Cruz, lead-on," Carol pronounced.

Carol and Lyle followed the officer. They took an elevator down to the main floor and went through a TSA gate that let them into a corridor behind the TSA passenger check stations.

The officer continued along the corridor and turned into an office. She signaled to Carol and Lyle to sit down and entered an adjoining office. In a few moments, she reappeared and waved them into the room. The officer stepped aside as Carol and Lyle entered. Once they were in the room, the woman departed, closing the door after herself.

A tall, neatly-bearded man with salt and pepper hair stood behind his desk. "Dr. Montgomery, Dr. Parnassus, thank you for coming in. Please, have a seat."

Lyle looked carefully at the man as he sat down. "Bill Sheridan…? What the hell are you doing here? I thought you had a class at the academy this year?"

"Lyle, nice to see you. I did have one, but it got rescheduled, and I got transferred. Hey, though, El Paso is much nicer in the winter than D.C. How was your flight?"

Carol looked at her husband, her brows creased with curiosity, and asked, "How do you two know one another? From your stint at Brown, Lyle?"

Both men laughed. "Yes, Bill was my co-instructor in our Diversity in Law class. He did the law part, and I did the diversity part."

Bill Sheridan spoke up, "Dr. Montgomery, it is a pleasure to meet you! Lyle had nothing but praise for you when we were teaching together. Sort of like him, I was on a sabbatical of sorts from the CIA. Hey, that reminds me, Lyle, how did the young Navajo man make out after he graduated?"

"He has done great and is prospering beyond anyone's expectations. He and that brilliant wife of his are an excellent team."

"That's great to hear. That young man, I don't remember his name – senior moment, I guess," he chuckled, "was just about the best student I've ever had dealings with. But we need to get to the reason for your visit to my office."

"Yes, that would be nice," Carol interjected. "I'm really tired, and we still have to drive to Cruces."

"Just a moment, please." Bill Sheridan pressed the key on his interoffice communicator, "Sally, can you and Charlie come in now, please?"

The office door opened, and two uniformed TSA officers entered.

"Dr. Montgomery – may I call you Carol? – may these folks inspect your cat carrier? I presume you can hold your cat on your lap."

*I have a bad feeling about this, as Han would say.*

**Be cool, my familiar. Let's see what this is all about.**

"Yes, and yes." Carol opened the carrier, and Rogue jumped out and onto her lap. She offered the carrier to the officers, who took it and left the room.

Bill looked quickly at Carol and Lyle and stated, "They will be right back, and I promise, they won't destroy the carrier – if they do, a new one will come out of their pay."

Carol looked at Lyle; the tension in the room was palpable.

"Okay, Bill, what's going on? Why the cat carrier, and why are we here?" Lyle asked, leaning slightly forward.

"Okay. Carol, you were in Morocco to help with decisions on stabilizing their mud monuments, right? And, Lyle, you went along to provide a male escort to avoid issues with some of their more conservative Imams, right?"

"Yes, and yes," Carol replied, "So?"

"Lyle, you got hooked up with some historians there that were looking for some very old writings thought to have been done by Mohammed himself. Is that right?"

"Yes, but it turned out that the things they were looking for and the stuff they found were not what they wanted."

"What did they find?"

"Some ancient, crumbly, parchment manuscripts fell out of a niche in the wall of one of the mud mosques that Carol was helping with. They proved to be a series of prayers from an almost unheard-of Imam who had been associated with that mosque. That Imam may have written the prayers as Mohammed dictated them — at least that's one of the ideas."

"What happened to those manuscripts?"

"Bill, I honestly don't know. They were given to the team leader looking for the Mohammed stuff, and he was supposed to pass them on to the government representative they were working with. I never really had my hands on the manuscript. I only saw it briefly after it dropped out of the wall niche — which is probably okay because I don't read Arabic. I was there when the team leader handed the parchment to the museum guy."

"You are sure that the museum person received the manuscript?"

"As sure as I'm human."

"Hmm… Carol, where was your cat carrier while you were in Marrakech?"

"It was in our room at the Riad where we stayed. Why?"

"In a moment — let me ask a couple more questions first. Did you ever see any evidence of anyone in your room when you were out?"

"Other than the maid service with the clean linens, no."

"You saw no evidence that anyone might have messed with or moved your cat carrier?"

"Not that I noticed," Carol replied, "although I suppose the maids may have shifted it while straightening the room."

The door opened; the two TSA officers came in and handed Carol the cat carrier. The young man looked at Bill, shook his head, and the pair left.

*That was weird.*

**Agreed – let's see where this is going.**

Bill Spencer leaned back in his office chair and stared at the ceiling for a few moments. Carol, Rogue, and Lyle sat and watched him… He straightened up, looked squarely at Carol, and smiled.

*I sense an excuse coming.*

***Your cat senses are highly tuned. I agree.***

"Well, Dr. Montgomery, Dr. Parnassus, it appears that we have gotten some bum information. As I expected, you are not international artifact thieves, but good, highly-trained professionals – an academician and an engineer. Carol, I have heard from my Moroccan connections that your work and help were exemplary and beyond reproach. Lyle, your handling of the manuscript's situation was also exemplary, and clearly, we now know, beyond reproach. I will report to my masters that their sources sent them on a wild goose chase. My apologies also to your cat — Rogue, isn't it?"

"So. There was nothing secreted into the carrier?"

*Of course not. I could have told the ding-dongs that. I am a highly-tuned cat, and that is my home away from home. Hmpff.*

"A little bit of cat hair in the bedding," Bill waved his hand as if to whisk away the question, "But, hey, I will be in Cruces on business in about a week; how about we get together for a glass of vino and some story-telling time? I really would like to hear more about your adventures, Carol."

"Sounds like a great idea, Bill. Thank you. Do take care, and enjoy El Paso," Lyle said as he and Carol stood. Rogue jumped off Carol's lap and into the carrier, which Carol closed and picked up.

*About time. Let's get out of here. I don't think I like this man.*

The young woman who had escorted Carol and Lyle came into the room and waved them out. The pair looked at one another and followed the young woman back into the terminal. The trio cleared the TSA area, and the young officer stopped and waved the two toward the baggage claim area.

"Bye, folks; have a safe drive home! There's a cab waiting outside. It will take you to your car," the young woman said and walked back toward the TSA office area. Carol and Lyle walked to the baggage claim area, which was largely empty, where they spotted their luggage off to the side of one of the belts with another young TSA officer standing nearby.

"Hi, are you Dr. Montgomery and Dr. Parnassus?"

"Yes, that would be us," Carol replied.

"Let me help you out to the cab with this luggage."

"Why, thank you very much. That will be appreciated."

*Carol, someone has fiddled with your luggage again. It doesn't smell right.*

***You are right. I see some clothes poking out. The customs people in Madrid and Dallas were much neater.***

# Chapter Three

Carol walked in the Camponotus Renovation office door with Rogue prancing along at her heels. Ami looked up from perusing the day's news briefs on her phone, did a double-take, then jumped up and gave Carol a huge abrazo. Carol returned the hug and then looked around the office.

Rogue pranced into the kitchenette and jumped onto the counter.

*Where's my breakfast? The place smells different. Ami is pudgy again.*

***You just had food, and you're the one that's getting pudgy — of course it smells different; you just got used to souks, Morocco, and airports.***

Carol stood in the center of the room and slowly looked around.

"Wow. You know, Ami, there were moments when I wasn't sure I would see this again."

"Really? Were things bad in Morocco?" Ami replied.

"No, not really bad in the danger sense, but confusing at times. I really loved the buildings, the people – well, most of them – and the country. So much of Morocco reminded me of places in New Mexico and the western U.S. - the desert parts, anyway."

"And how did that make you think you wouldn't be back?"

"I had several offers of really super-nice positions with some European-based companies and a department in the Moroccan government. The temptation was strong, and the money was tremendous, but… well, this is my company, and I do things my way."

"So, I take it this means you are glad to be home?"

"Indeed I am, Ami. As is Rogue. She was not as enamored with Morocco as I was. While she had some cat friends, there was an old witch, a Sahira, in one of the souks with a cat familiar… they didn't get along at all."

"Souks? Is that what they call the markets?"

"Yes, it is. Narrow alleys, crowds of people, zillions of shops. Overall, fascinating."

"How did you come across a witch?"

"Interesting story – best kept for an evening of wine and barbeque. But, the short version is my fascination with fortune-tellers. I went into the Sahira's parlor; she immediately knew I was a witch and Rogue was my familiar. She never cottoned on to the telepathy, however. The Sahira's familiar was an old, scrawny black tom cat – like you see in the cartoons. He was grumpy and immediately disliked Rogue, which, needless to say, was mutual."

*That flea-bitten, scrawny old tom was critical to the Sahira. The cat fairly glowed with arcane powers. The Sahira's powers were diminished whenever he wasn't nearby. I detested him, but he was her familiar, and he absolutely doted on the old woman. At least he was a cat – not a bird – like that mynah of Roger's.*

*I thought you and Basil had learned to like one another?*

*Tolerate is maybe the better word. Cats like birds – for lunch.*

**Hmm – Rogue, you are a brat.**

Ami looked at Carol, "What are you and Rogue arguing about now?"

"Bygones and agreeing on the story. Anyway, the old Sahira, Aliyah, which means wonderful or miracle in Arabic, proved to be very helpful in locating some ancient documents hidden in one of the damaged mosques. We found those for the team of historians, antiquities specialists, and manuscript students Lyle had hooked up with. The group was formed by UNESCO, as was my group of engineers after the big quakes ruined many of Morocco's historic mud mosques and castles. There were rumors of hidden manuscripts written by Mohammed in one of the mosques. Supposedly, the manuscripts we found went to the government-run Islamic Museum."

"Supposedly?"

"That's another story that may not have an ending yet. We got shaken down in El Paso by the TSA and CIA looking for the missing manuscripts. They found nothing – which is the correct answer — but I'm not convinced that they are convinced. Anyway, tell me more about the guy who wants me to engineer the corner of his house."

"Now, having heard your tale about Moroccan manuscripts, I am getting suspicious. The dude is from the Arabic world somewhere. He could be Moroccan. I can't separate their accents worth a damn. He has been clanging my cage bars daily since his first call. You being delayed getting home appears to have rattled his cage. He's supposed to come by this morning sometime after ten. I'll let you decide what you think."

"Hmm – I need to talk to Lyle when he gets home from his office. His classes start next week, and he had a meeting this morning with the Dean. I think we may have been followed home last night, and I noticed a cop-cruiser-looking car down the street when I walked over to the office. What do we know about the house? Anything more than what we knew when we talked to the previous owner?"

"No, nothing solid. I did chat with one of the daughters of the previous owner. I was curious why they sold. She regaled me with a story about a man in a gray duster, an old style of overcoat — a ghost who lives in the house and turns up every now and again, usually somewhere near the fireplace in the dining room. Usually makes his appearance on nasty, cold, windy days."

"Now that's interesting. You say the daughter had seen the ghost?"

"Oh, yes. In fact, the daughter says she talked to him when she was young. He seemed harmless and had never done anything but look sad and gray. It annoyed her mom a lot, so they had the house exorcised. The daughter said she has not seen the gray man since."

"Hmm — Okay, let's see what we have on the schedule — there is a schedule, right?"

The office phone rang, and Ami picked it up. "Yessir, she's here now. I'll give her the phone." She pushed the hold button on the phone and placed it back in the cradle. "Carol, it's the good Mr. Percival seeking your counsel."

Carol looked sideways at Ami, laughed, sat at her desk, and picked up the phone, "Hello, Mr. Percival. Yes, this is Dr. Montgomery. I'm sorry for the delay. We had a lash-up with our flight home – had to lay over an extra couple of nights in Madrid. I believe there was a tornado in Texas or a hurricane in Florida. What can I do for you?"

Carol listened, then responded, "Yes, Mr. Percival. That is correct. I have been involved with that house. The building does not have a concrete footing. It was built entirely on wooden jack posts, mostly replaced over time with concrete supports. Yes, they do make special hydraulic jacks that can be installed on the bedrock or, in this area, the caliche layer, which will prevent further settling. I do not do that work myself, but I have a contact in Albuquerque who specializes in fixing settling buildings."

Carol listened for a bit longer, then responded, "Yes, sir. Basically, that requires crawling under the house and jacking up the joists in the sagging area, then placing fixed jacks or concrete blocks to support the floor...how about two-ish this afternoon? I have some things to catch up on in the office, and then I will be available. Stuff does pile up after being gone for over a month ... Very good. See you about two. Thank you. Bye."

Carol set the phone back on the hook, stood up, stretched, and said, "That guy is pushy. I'll have no problem giving him to the guys from up north. Okay, now let's look at the schedule."

Ami shook her head and pulled a folder from her desk drawer.

"Here's what I've saved for you, boss lady. Read 'em and weep. Or rejoice – your choice. Besides the good Mr. Percival, you have the City Planners, the Historic Preservation Committee folks, and Detective Sanchez all seeking your brilliance and beauty. A developer is preparing to destroy the old adobe clubhouse on the city's defunct golf course property. Hence, the Hysterical folks and the Planners."

# Chapter Four

The small, swarthy man stood on the curb outside the stone wall as Carol and Ami pulled up in Carol's truck.

"Good afternoon, you must be Dr. Montgomery and Ms. Lopez," the man said as the women stepped onto the sidewalk.

Carol stepped forward, "Yes, I'm Dr. Montgomery. You would be Mr. Percival, yes?"

George Percival responded, "Yes, yes, you are correct. It is good to meet you at last." Turning to Ami, he said, "And, therefore, you would be Ms. Lopez. I have enjoyed talking to you. It is so good to deal with professional people."

"Thank you, Mr. Percival." Ami began. "But now, we should look at your problem and let Dr. Montgomery review the situation and see what, if anything, has changed. As you know, Dr. Montgomery looked at this issue some while ago."

"Yes, yes. Of course. Please do come in," George Percival opened the gate and waved the women through.

Carol walked immediately to the southwest corner of the house, got on her knees, and carefully examined the siding that enclosed the footing. She dug a small handful of soil from the small, walled flower bed surrounding the corner and sifted it through her hand. Carol sat for a moment in thought, then stood up.

"May we go inside now, please?"

"Of course. Follow me," George Percival led the women back to the porch. The front door was standing open.

He waved the women into the house. Carol turned left into the dining room and stopped in front of the fireplace, which contained a small electric log. She looked carefully at the brickwork, running her hand lightly over the brick supports for the mantle. Carol then turned around and walked around the table and into the corner of the room – the southwest corner of the house. Kneeling down, she could plainly see the southwest-trending slope in the floor and noted residue from a recent spill.

"Mr. Percival, have you ever been under the house?"

"Why no, Dr. Montgomery. Why do you ask?"

"There used to be a gas floor heater in the entryway, and next to it was a hatch for access to the crawl space. The previous owners removed the furnace and put a heat pump on the roof. They apparently closed off access to the crawl space. I wonder how workmen will get to the corner to jack it up and install supports."

"Hmm, Dr. Montgomery, I was unaware of that. Is there no access from the rear of the house?"

"I believe there is. However, the central supporting joist, which is a large beam, as I recall from my prior inspection, makes getting over to the southwest corner something only a snake or a skinny kid can do without digging a trench."

"Oh my, what do you suggest?"

"Well, I noted that the fireplace shows some evidence of settling. It might be well to consider reinforcing that area and the corner. I believe that the crawl space can be accessed from the fireplace. Opening the floor of the fireplace and the hearth would allow both repairs to be done. It will be a bit of an inconvenience and a mess, but I suspect that if you don't do something like that, you will lose this corner of the house."

"Is it really quite that dire, Dr. Montgomery?"

"Yes, I believe it is. The house, overall, is structurally sound and solid. However, the southwest corner lies over what I think is a clay lens. The flowerbed there has contributed water to the clay and caused swelling. The previous owners noted that and stopped planting anything in that bed. The soil today is very dry. When the bed stopped receiving water, the clay shrunk and contributed to the settling. The clay lens can be addressed by putting a deep hydraulic jack under the corner, extending below the clay, and providing a stable and long-term solution."

"But will that work? And what about the rest of the structure under this area?"

"I have seen a similar situation on the west side of Las Cruces in the old river channel area. The jacks have been in place for about ten years, and there has been no further evidence of subsidence. Stabilizing the corner will allow regular short jacks or concrete blocks to be installed under the rest of the room. That should deal with the current unevenness of the floor and stabilize the fireplace, which is a beautiful piece of brickwork."

"Oh my gosh. That's a lot to ponder, Dr. Montgomery. May I think about this, talk to my wife, and consult with my bank, then get back to you?"

"Certainly, take as much time as you need. This house is a classic from the early twentieth century and worth the effort. In fact, there may be some State funds available through the City because this is a historic district."

"Thank you, Dr. Montgomery and Ms. Lopez. Is there anything else? If not, may I see you to the door? I don't mean to be rude, but I am expecting a business associate."

"Here is Dr. Montgomery's business card, Mr. Percival. Let us know what you decide," Ami said as she handed the card to the man.

Carol and Ami left the house, closed the gate, and began to drive west on Hadley. As they pulled away, Carol noticed a dark sedan pull up to the curb in front of the house. At the same time, she saw a gray cop cruiser turn onto Hadley from Virginia Street. When she turned south onto Campo, Carol checked her rear-view mirror – the gray cruiser was turning onto the same road as her.

"Didn't you say Xochitl wanted to talk to me?" Carol asked Ami.

"Uhh – yes – I did. She called the day before you got back."

"It's time to pay her a visit," Carol said, turning west onto Las Cruces Avenue.

The cruiser followed . Carol turned north onto Water Street, then east onto Hadley Avenue once again before driving north on Campo. Shortly after, she crossed Picacho Avenue, and pulled into the Police Department parking lot. The cruiser in turn ducked east on Picacho Avenue and disappeared around a bend in the street.

"What's going on, Carol?"

"We are being followed. Gray cruiser-type car. I wanted to spook them. Pulling into the cop shop might help resolve who they are working for… Let's go inside and see if Detective Sanchez is home."

# Chapter Five

Detective Xochitl Sanchez gave Carol and Ami each a big abrazo, closed her office door, and the women sat down around a small conference table.

"Carol, it's wonderful to see you. How's Rogue and that handsome husband of yours?"

"We're all good and happy to be home. How are things in your patch?"

"Ah, well – cop work is cop work – what else can I say?" With a wave of her hand, she whisked the subject away in favor of the next, "Ami, how's that new grandson?"

"Granddaughter. Wonderful — but how did you know about her?"

"Ami, the walls have eyes and ears. One of my cousins works at Mountain View in the O.B. ward. She told me about Anthony and Trish's bit of flurry when the baby was born. I'm really happy to hear she is good."

"Ami, you didn't tell me that Trish had given birth – but hey, I should have figured it out – nine months and all that," Carol interjected.

"So, Carol, let me guess – you want to know why I called and asked to speak to you."

"Well, that and a query about why a gray cop-cruiser is bird-dogging me."

"Ah, yes. Figured you might have questions. Listen, I can't really say much about what's going on. Top drawer and all that, you know."

"I see," Carol replied, looking directly at Xochitl. "Okay, how about we get together at that little coffee shop on Mesquite for donuts and a mug? I'll regale you with our adventures in the land of souks, caravanserais, and mud kasbahs."

"Capital idea, Carol. I'm off in a half-hour. But that coffee shop closed, so how about the place across from the college."

"Sounds muy bueno, Xochitl. See you there in about an hour. I need to run by the office and see if hubby-bubby is home from his meeting yet."

"Yes, and I need to get my buns home. Iggy is due home early today – which means he'll be gone tonight," Ami added.

"Great! I'll see you and maybe Lyle at Milagro at about five-thirty, assuming I don't get hijacked by work. Maybe supper after we b.s. – what do you think?"

"For sure. Hasta, then."

Carol and Ami got up and left. Xochitl picked up her office phone and selected a number.

"Okay, Carol, what gives? I detected some code words in that conversation," Ami asked as the women pulled out of the police parking lot.

Carol watched her rear-view mirror as she turned out of the station, headed west. The gray cruiser was there.

"Ami, we are being followed again. Xochitl couldn't talk in her office but will tell me what she can over coffee. I hope she can talk to me then – I suspect our followers may dampen the spirit of the b.s. session."

"Gee, what fun. Okay, drop me at the office, and you and Lyle get together with Xochitl. I'm going to put the squeeze on Iggy. There's a good chance he knows something about what's happening."

"That sounds good, Ami. See you tomorrow — early?"

"If early means after eight, then sí."

Ami climbed out of the truck and headed for her car. Carol locked the truck and entered the office; emerging a few minutes later, she walked across the yard to her home. The gray cruiser was parked down the street. Rogue bounded out of the kitchen cat door and rubbed Carol's legs.

*Boss, where have you been? I thought I had lost you. You are worried silly, which is stirring up my cat's gray cells.*

***Had an appointment, my familiar. Yes, I'm worried. Lyle and I need to meet Xochitl at the coffee shop in about a half hour.***

*Oh, boy. Can I come? I like that Barista – she gives me half-and-half, which is almost as good as cream.*

***Milk is reputedly not good for cats, but sure, why not? You are my support cat, after all. Is Lyle home?***

*Yes, he's in the kitchen staring around hungrily. Speaking of hungry . . .*

Carol opened the kitchen door, walked in, and hugged her husband.

"Hey, hello. What's up? I haven't eaten since breakfast and was trying to find grub," Lyle said, returning Carol's hug.

"We are supposed to meet Xochitl at Milagro in about a half hour. How about a snack then and supper later? Xochitl did mumble something about supping together."

*Hey, how about me? I haven't eaten since the last time I ate.*

**Hang tough, gata. I'll get you a little container of half-and-half at Milagro.**

"Did you notice a gray cop-cruiser-looking car when you drove up?" Carol asked her husband.

"No, is there one out there now?"

"There was when I came across from the office. It's been bird-dogging me all day. I'm hoping Xochitl can shed some light on it."

"Hmm – that's interesting. I thought I saw a follower myself, coming back from my meeting at the U."

"Lyle, this stinks. It has something to do with those manuscripts, I'm sure. What the hell do you think is going on?"

"I don't know, but let's meet Xochitl and see what we can find out. I'm guessing she couldn't talk at her office? I presume that's where you went."

"Yes, after we met with the guy at the house on Hadley, we drove by the cop shop. Xochitl had called Ami the other day and said she wanted to chat. Oh, yeah – Ami is going to rag on Iggy and see if he knows anything."

"Sounds like a good idea. Okay, let's go. Is her-meowness coming?"

"Yes, she is begging for half-and-half, and that Barista at Milagro likes her."

Carol, Lyle, and Rogue walked to Carol's truck. Carol backed out of her office driveway and gazed down the street. The gray cruiser was not there, but a pale blue Mazda was parked along the curb.

"Lyle, what did your follower look like?"

"Hmm – a light blue sporty-car of some kind. I didn't get a real good look."

"Like that one along the curb, there?"

"Yepper."

"Okay, let's see if they are now also my followers. The cruiser is not around, that I can see."

Carol accelerated down the street, turned sharply at the next corner, and pulled quickly behind the store on the corner. The blue Mazda zipped by. As she started to pull back out, the gray cruiser came around the further corner and pulled onto Carol's street. As soon as it was out of sight, Carol pulled a U-turn and turned away from her house at the corner. She turned onto a side street, then back onto the main street. The cruiser, followed by the Mazda, zipped past, going in the other direction. Carol turned at the next intersection and headed toward downtown. When she reached University Avenue, she turned towards I-10, then onto Main. A short distance along Main, Carol turned onto a short cul de sac, made the loop, and returned toward University Avenue. Carol turned onto University Avenue, pulled into one of the university's parking lots, into a space facing the street, and shut off the truck. Lyle and Rogue said nothing. Lyle gave his wife a look. The gray cruiser and the blue Mazda motored past, heading toward the Milagro Coffee Shop. Carol took her phone from her purse and dialed a number.

"Xochitl, we are being bird-dogged by two cars. I am stashed in a parking lot, but the followers are headed toward Milagro. We'll meet you at Comida de Camino in a few minutes. Take the roundabout route. Bye."

The gray cruiser returned along University Avenue and pulled into the lot, parking several cars away from Carol. Someone got out of the car and walked toward the truck.

"Be very quiet, no matter what happens," Carol said as she locked the truck's doors and mumbled the disappearance spell.

The person from the cruiser walked past the back of Carol's truck, stepped onto the sidewalk, and then back along the sidewalk, slowing to stare fixedly at the vehicle. The cab of the truck appeared empty. Still, the person walked right up to it and peered intently into the windows. There was nothing to be seen, except some very light indentations of the seats, which the person did not notice. Shaking their head, the person returned to their car, got in, and left.

Carol, Lyle, and Rogue remained still and silent. When the cruiser had been gone for several minutes, Carol mumbled a spell, and the three reappeared in the truck. Carol started the truck, pulled out of the parking lot, and headed toward Mesilla. She watched her mirror carefully. No cruiser and no Mazda appeared. Carol drove into Mesilla and wandered about on the narrow streets before pulling into the parking lot next to the Basilica of San Albino, the historic cathedral of Mesilla.

"I'm going to park here. Lyle, we can walk to the Comida de Camino; it's just around the corner. Rogue, I want you to stay here with the truck and let me know if anyone comes snooping around."

*What about my treat? You promised.*

***Faithful familiar, I will buy you a case of half-and-half if that will make you feel better. I need your sharp kitty-cat eyes and ears working for me right now.***

*Hmm—okay—I'll stay right here. If I sit on that wall around the lot, I'll just look like another of the local stray cats. When we get home, a small cup of half-and-half will be fine.*

***Great, thank you. It'll be about an hour. I suspect Xochitl will want to eat something and chin-wag. If you need to, you can hide under the truck.***

*Be careful, my witch.*

# Chapter Six

Lyle and Carol found a table near the back of the patio, under a tree, with a clear view of the gate. The Comida de Camino had, for years, been Josefina's Green Gate. It was known for its great posole and a nice patio in a walled yard. Xochitl and another woman walked through the gate, stood momentarily looking, and continued back to Carol and Lyle's table.

"Carol, Lyle – how good to see you. This is my good friend and companion, Lobelia Trent. She has taken over from my dog as my bed warmer and source of abrazos when things get tough. Where's Rogue?"

The two stood, and Carol responded, "Xochitl, good to see you. Lobelia, how very nice to meet you. It is great that Xochitl now has someone to attach to who is human. Please sit down. We haven't ordered yet, but I'm dying to try their posole and see if it's as good as Josefina's."

Xochitl and Lobelia took chairs across from Carol and Lyle. Xochitl stretched and gazed around the patio.

"Carol, I don't see anyone interesting. Can we talk?"

"Is Lobelia okay?" asked Carol.

"Yes, she is my confidant, among other things. She's a 911 dispatcher for the county and has been trained to be discreet."

Lobelia said nothing but smiled.

"Did you see a gray cruiser or a blue Mazda at Milagro?" Lyle asked.

"We never got to Milagro," Xochitl replied. I got sidetracked by a work-related hoo-haw and then had to scuffle to get home and change. Carol's message found me at home.

"Hmm. A blue Mazda is following Lyle, and the gray cruiser I mentioned to you is following me. Based on how they responded as we headed for Milagro, they are hooked up."

"What did they do," Lobelia asked, "if I may be so bold?"

"The Mazda was watching the house when we left. The cruiser joined the chase a couple of blocks away as I was maneuvering to avoid the Mazda. I did manage to toss both of them, and we got a very good look at the cruiser driver."

"How did you do that?" asked Xochitl.

"I was in a university parking lot when I messaged you. The cruiser saw my truck and pulled into the lot. We were not there when he came up and stared into the cab."

Lobelia looked at Carol and then at Xochitl. "Umm, excuse my ignorance, but if you were not there, how did you get a good look at the person?"

"Long story, Lobelia – but I'm Wiccan."

"Oh, I see – well, I guess I see."

"Lobelia, my love, I'll 'splain it all in detail later," Xochitl responded.

"Xochitl, what do you know about all of this? I assume you have some knowledge since it looks like CIA or FBI, and you have those connections," Carol asked.

"Actually, Carol, Lyle – not very much. My contact in Albuquerque alerted me and requested that I say nothing. I think it has something to do with ancient artifact smuggling. Something Lyle was involved with in Morocco."

"Hmm," Lyle responded, "The TSA shook us down in El Paso when we landed but found nothing — or so they say. The fact is, I have no artifacts, ancient or otherwise, but apparently, someone is not convinced."

"Hey, here comes the waiter; let's order and eat. I, for one, am starved," Xochitl pointed toward the gate.

*Hey boss – someone's snooping around the truck. Looks sort of like the person we saw in the parking lot.*

***Thanks, Rogue. Some suspicious-looking folks just walked onto the patio. We are gonna order, eat, and get gone.***

Two people in suits, a stern man and a woman wearing a hijab, walked through the gate and looked around. Carol and Lyle hid behind their menus. The two strangers turned around and exited the patio.

"What can I get you folks," the waiter asked as he walked up to the table.

"How's the posole today?" asked Carol. "Is it as good as Josefina used to serve?"

"Yes, ma'am, it is. We actually hired Josefina's chef."

"Excellent. I'll have a bowl of posole with a flour tortilla and a Negra Modelo," Carol responded.

"Same for me," Xochitl stated

"Me too," Lyle answered.

"Me three," Lobelia responded.

The waiter chuckled as he noted their order, thanked them, and walked inside.

*Boss, two more people just showed up, and they're all talking. The new ones look sort of like Feds. I'll drift over there and see if I can pick up on their conversation.*

**Be careful, my faithful familiar. Don't get caught or squashed.**

*Boss, you know they will ignore a cat, even one rubbing on their gray suit pants legs.*

Carol chuckled, and Xochitl gave her a look, "What's that about?"

"The spooks found my truck. Rogue is listening in on the spooks' conversation and rubbing cat hair onto their suit pants legs."

Lobelia gave the two women a puzzled expression, "Whaat?"

Lyle, Carol, and Xochitl laughed, and Xochitl said, "Lobelia, I'll 'splain all later. Right now, here comes our beer."

*Boss, the woman reached down to scratch my ears, so I scurried under the truck. The gray suits are speaking English and what sounds like Arabic to the two men from the Mazda. They don't seem to know much English.*

*The four of them have put three tracking devices on the truck. The Arabic speakers put two, and the gray suits one. I, of course, know where they all are hidden.*

**Great job so far, Rogue. Let me know when they leave. The server is just now bringing our posole. We should be ready to head home in about half an hour. Can you stay hidden till then?**

*Of course, my witch. It's actually kind of nice under the truck.*

*Oh... I think they're all leaving. I will check in a few minutes. Enjoy your posole. I'm going to love the half-and-half.*

"My spy is keeping an eye on things. She says the spooks are leaving. Wow, this is good posole," Carol said as she spooned up some of her soup, loaded with cilantro, onions, and a squeeze of lime juice.

"Wish I had a spy like that," Xochitl remarked. "Mmm — yes. Every bit as good as Josefina's."

Lyle folded a tortilla, tore it into four triangles, rolled one, dipped a spoonful of his posole, and took a bite of the rolled tortilla. "Sure wasn't anything like this in Marrakech."

"Tell me more about Marrakech," Lobelia asked. "I have long hankered to visit the famed souks and whirling dervishes."

"Souks we visited — dervishes are not in Morocco — that Islamic tradition is apparently only found in Türkiye — that's Turkey's official name," Carol interjected. "Kasbahs and mosques made of mud and stone are abundant — at least before the quakes. Way too many of them are now piles of dirt and rocks. I'm not sure the Moroccan government can ever rebuild many of those. Our specialist group pointed to ways to fix or salvage some of the most important ones, but the lesser ones — I just don't know."

"Yes, that mosque where the manuscripts turned up was a mess. That ancient manuscript may have disappeared forever if it wasn't for that old witch that Carol hooked up with," Lyle contributed. "Though," he went on with some apprehension, "based on what's happening here and now, there's... Well, there may be reasonable suspicion it did actually disappear forever this time."

*They have well and truly left, boss. They think their tracking gizmos will keep them informed about your whereabouts.*

***Hmm — well, we'll have to see about that. We are nearly finished with supper. Should be there soon.***

The quartet finished their posoles and drank the last of their beers. Lyle picked up the tab, not without some wrangling with Xochitl. Lobelia and Xochitl turned toward the Plaza and the parking area in front of the Basilica. Lyle and Carol crossed the street, headed for the lot on the other side of the Basilica.

"So, tracking devices. Hmm – now, what can we do to foil their plans?" Carol queried as they walked to the truck.

"How about we put the devices on other vehicles? You said three devices, right?"

"That's right. Hee hee – my truck going in three different directions. That should twist their heads. Okay – let's do it."

As the pair walked into the parking lot, the priest from the Basilica climbed out of his car, nodded politely toward the pair, and hurried toward the church. Carol and Lyle looked at one another and walked faster. Rogue pranced out from under the truck as they approached.

*Hey Boss. I've been keeping watch from the wall. No sign of your friends returning.*

***Great. You have earned your half-and-half twice over. Now, will you show us where the tracking devices are located?***

Rogue meowed quietly and stopped under the rear bumper. Carol felt around and found the small magnetically attached device and pulled it off the bumper. Looking around, Carol saw no one anywhere nearby. She walked to the priest's car and stuck the device under his rear bumper.

Rogue went under the truck and stopped under the left front fender. Carol felt around until she found the device and removed it. As Carol stood up from removing the tracking device, a city Dial-A-Ride bus stopped just outside the parking lot, and the driver walked across the street to a residence. Carol sauntered over to the bus and stuck the device just under the right headlight.

While Carol was attaching her find to the bus, Lyle recovered the remainder from the right front fender well of the truck. He lodged the tracker into the left front fender well of the car parked alongside their vehicle. Carol opened her driver-side door, and climbed in just as the bus driver and an elderly woman entered the bus. The Dial-A-Ride's doors were closed, and it pulled away. Lyle climbed into the passenger seat, and Rogue jumped onto Carol's shoulder. Carol started the engine, grinned broadly at Lyle, scratched Rogue's belly, and drove off.

A few blocks away, the blue Mazda tucked in behind the city bus. The driver and passenger looked at one another, then cursed in Arabic. The gray cruiser sat along a street near the Plaza. After about two hours, the cruiser drove around to the parking lot. The truck was gone, but the tracking signal emanated from the lot. A brief search led the cruiser's occupants to the priest's car just as he emerged from the church, walked across the street, and drove away. Some folks entering the parking lot were treated to loud, profane exclamations in both English and Arabic.

# Chapter Seven

Carol looked up from reading her computer screen as Ami walked in the door.

"How did your coffee and supper with Xochitl go?" Ami asked as she dropped her purse into her desk drawer.

"Well, we didn't actually do the coffee, but we did have a great bowl of posole at Comida de Camino. Xochitl has a new friend, bed warmer, and back massager. Her name is Lobelia Trent. Very bright and very nice."

"Well, that's great. I am happy for Xochitl, and for Lobelia. Was Xochitl able to add anything about what's happening?"

"Not really. Only that her FBI connection in Albuquerque called and said to say nothing."

"Hmm – that, in itself, is suspicious."

"Does Iggy know anything?"

"Well, yes and no. There is some sort of foo-faw from the Feds, but nothing specific. The best he can tell me is that someone thinks Lyle swung with some ancient manuscript. Iggy has no idea why or what the fuss is about."

"We are really not getting much help at all in this mess. My followers put tracking devices on my truck while we were eating. Rogue watched them, and when we returned to the truck, the devices magically appeared on other vehicles. I suspect there were a few choice words when the followers discovered that."

"Ah-ha, the Wiley Witch of the West strikes again," Ami responded with a laugh. "Okay. Let's see. I got an email from Mr. Percival early this morning. He wants to come by the office this afternoon and formalize a contract. You have a meeting at City Hall with the Hysterical Committee folks at six this afternoon. The new Mayor wants to chat and suggested about four this afternoon. I suspect his chat will have something to do with the Historic Preservation Committee meeting."

"All right. I need to call the guy in Albuquerque and see if and when he can come down to look at Percival's problem. Please draw up a draft contract for the corner stabilization and fireplace repair. Leave the money open until I get something from the engineers up north. I'm going to have to get the information on what the developer wants to do at the old golf course. What do we know about that adobe clubhouse?"

⌂ ⌂ ⌂

"Mr. Percival, come in. Let's park on the couch where we can talk more comfortably," Carol said, inviting the man into the office. "Can I offer you anything to drink? Water? Tea? Coffee?"

"Thank you, Dr. Montgomery, but actually, I would feel more comfortable in a chair at your desk. And, yes, a cup of tea would be wonderful."

"Ami, will you be so kind as to get Mr. Percival a cup of tea? I think the water should still be hot enough. Mr. Percival, I can offer you Earl Grey, Darjeeling, or English Teatime."

"English Teatime would be splendid, Dr. Montgomery. Thank you."

Ami stepped back into the kitchenette, the whistle of the kettle boiling and the clatter of teacups was heard not long after. In a moment, she re-emerged with a small tray with three cups, a fancy teapot, a sugar bowl, and creamer. Ami set a cup in front of Carol, another in front of Mr. Percival, and the third on her desk, then began to fill each. She offered the sugar and creamer to Mr. Percival, who waved them away. Neither Carol nor Ami used cream or sugar. Ami set the teapot on a side table and returned to her desk.

"So, Dr. Montgomery, have you prepared a contract for the work we discussed?"

"Indeed, I have, Mr. Percival. It is in draft form because I am waiting for the engineering company in Albuquerque to get back to me with an estimate. The lead engineer wishes to re-inspect the situation before he provides a final bid. He says he will be in Las Cruces tomorrow. Would that be convenient for you?"

"Re-inspect?"

"Yes, sir. He made an estimate for the previous owner about two years ago."

"Hmm. All right. Yes, tomorrow will be fine. Any idea what time of day?"

"Not precisely, but probably about noon. It takes about three to four hours to drive down, and he will likely leave at about eight. Shall we tentatively say one o'clock? That will allow him some slack for traffic and a bite of lunch."

"Very well, one o'clock. Now, may I see the draft contract?"

"Of course. Ami, will you give the contract to Mr. Percival, please?"

Ami handed a thin sheaf of papers to Mr. Percival. The three sat quietly and drank their tea as George Percival read over the contract. While reading, he looked up a couple of times, a more or less quizzical expression on his face. When he finished reading, he took a large swallow of tea and looked squarely at Carol.

"Dr. Montgomery, the contract is a bit irregular in a couple of places, but I can find no fault. Barring the engineering company's estimate, your cost looks more than reasonable. I do, however, wonder about the historical review."

"Certainly, Mr. Percival. The work on the corner will require a building permit. Because the house is in the Mesquite Street - Original Townsite Historic District, approval of a building permit normally requires the approval of the Historical Preservation Committee. In this case, since changes will not be made to the exterior that are visible from the street, their approval will not be required.

However, the Historic Preservation Committee will want as much information regarding the home's history as we can find. Having them on our side is always a good idea — especially if you decide to make exterior, visible modifications in the future. Having a neat little historic package for the house will smooth whatever bumps might be in the process. I can provide the report at a reasonable price because my husband is on the history faculty at NMSU and has grad students who can do the legwork and prepare the report. It helps both the students and the Committee's staff."

"Ah, okay, yes, I see. Very efficient of you, Dr. Montgomery. I will see you then tomorrow at one, and we can, I hope, finalize the contract shortly thereafter."

Carol then rose from her chair and stepped around the desk. "Indeed, yes. Mr. Percival. Now, I don't want to run you off, but I have a meeting with the mayor that I need to do a little homework for."

"Okay, understood, Dr. Montgomery. Thank you." Percival stood, nodded to Carol, touched his forehead to Ami, and departed.

Carol and Ami looked at one another, smiled broadly, and Ami remarked, "Stuffy little shit, isn't he." Both women giggled, then sat back at their desks.

⌂ ⌂ ⌂

"Lyle, do you have a grad student that would like to make a few bucks? I want a search on ownership, etc., for that house at the corner of Espina and East Hadley. I want to get a leg up and avoid any unnecessary foo-faw with the permit."

"Yes, I do. I have a brand-new master's student who needs to start learning the ropes of historical research. Should I have her contact you?"

"Yes, please do. Have her email or text me. I have a meeting this afternoon with both the Mayor and the Historic Preservation Committee. So — how's your day going?"

"So far, quiet, but I've been summoned to the Dean's office right after lunch. I don't know what it's about, but I suspect something concerning the Moroccan manuscript."

"Well, crap. I wonder when that b.s. is going to settle?"

"Me three – it is getting old – especially since I have no idea what happened to the manuscript after it was handed to the government guy in Marrakech."

"Keep smilin', love. It makes the bastards wonder what you are up to."

"See you at home about six, then?"

"Probably later – maybe seven-ish or eight-ish – my meeting with the hysterical folks is at six."

"Okay. I'll burn something for supper – how's that sound?"

"Mmm, mmm, good. Love you. Bye, now."

Carol clicked her phone off and went back to reading the newspaper articles about the golf course development on her laptop. After about ten minutes, she looked up and asked, "Ami, are there no plans or papers from the developer that we can access?"

"Not that I've been able to find, Carol. That would be something to ask the mayor. Based on what I've seen in the paper, the developer may be trying to pull a fast one to avoid maintaining the Clubhouse."

"Hmm. Okay, I'll rattle the mayor's cage. How about information on the state of the building?"

"Again, I've not found anything recent. It was built in the twenties by some well-known local architect and hasn't been used, officially, for about five years – since they closed the golf course. Rumor has it that vagrants are camping there. You probably need to arrange a visit."

"Gee, what fun. I'll see if I can wrangle a visit. I suppose I have to go through the developer-slash-owner, or does the city still have any hooks into the building?"

"I think the city still has ownership or at least access. Let me call the city manager and see what I can work out."

"Okay – well then, I have read what I can find. It seems to be time to beard the dragon at City Hall." Carol stood up, put her phone in her back pocket, a folder of newspaper clippings in her briefcase, and left. Rogue pranced out the door right behind her.

Ami, in the meantime, dialed the city manager. His phone went to an answering machine, so she left a voice message and hung up. Ami leaned back in her chair and stared at the ceiling. *Now what? This is going to be an interesting time, a la the ancient Chinese saying. Weird guy with a house corner problem. Developer that could give a shit about historical structures. Hmmm.*

⌂ ⌂ ⌂

Carol parked in front of the City Hall, and she and Rogue went in. Carol went directly to the mayor's office, signed in on the appointment sheet, and sat down next to a burly man who appeared to be a developer – jeans with a pressed crease and a starched and pressed cotton shirt. The receptionist's phone beeped, and she picked up the receiver.

"Dr. Montgomery, Mr. Arthur, the Mayor will see you now."

Carol and the man next to her stood up. He signaled her to go ahead, and the pair, with Rogue, entered the mayor's office, closing the door as they entered. The mayor stood up and waved them toward a small conference table. The three found chairs at the table as Rogue jumped onto Carol's lap. The man who sat in a chair opposite Carol stared briefly at Rogue.

Looking straight at the man, Carol said, "The cat - her name is Rogue - is my companion cat. She is duly registered as such and accompanies me nearly everywhere."

Rogue meowed lightly. The man shook his head and turned his attention to the mayor.

*I don't like this guy. He's too neat and stiff. Pressed jeans, for crying out loud. Nobody presses jeans.*

***Developers do. They think it makes them look professional and casual at the same time. I agree with your assessment. Let's see where this goes.***

The mayor started the discussion, "Dr. Montgomery, this is Mr. Arthur of the golf course development group. Mr. Arthur, Dr. Montgomery.

Mr. Arthur, as you have probably been told, Dr. Montgomery is a structural engineer who specializes in adobe buildings. In fact, I understand that she just got back from Morocco, where she was on a team trying to help the government deal with the renovation or recovery of the many adobe and stone buildings that were damaged in the earthquakes a few months ago."

"Dr. Montgomery, very good to meet you. Your expertise is lauded in Las Cruces and the State's southern portion," Mr. Arthur said, offering Carol his hand.

Carol shook Mr. Arthur's hand and replied, "Mr. Arthur. My pleasure, I'm sure. However, I must admit, sir, that your company and expertise are virtually unknown in our city. Can you provide me a brief sketch of who you are and what your development plan for the old golf course is? To date. I have seen no paperwork indicating where you are going or what you plan to do - other than the newspaper accounts."

*Go get 'im, boss.*

"You do not fool around, do you, Doctor? Yes, of course. In fact, I have the development plan, in bound form, here in my briefcase." The man opened his briefcase and removed three spiral-bound copies of a report with a flashy cover page. He handed a copy of the report to the mayor and to Carol. The woman looked at the cover and then opened the report to the table of contents, which she quickly perused.

"Hmm. Mr. Arthur, I see nothing in the contents to indicate that you have any plan for saving or renovating the old clubhouse. Is that correct, or did I overlook something?"

"You are correct, Dr. Montgomery. We intend to raze the building to make room for a small mall-type complex in that location. I understand that the building has no official historic designation, so if I am not mistaken, there is no reason why we cannot follow through on that action."

"Carol, Mr. Arthur is correct. Although the historical society folks have been trying to get the building designated, they have not been successful," the mayor interjected.

"Yes, that is what I gleaned from the newspaper stories, Bill. Mr. Arthur, in the interest of historic preservation, may I get permission to investigate the building – perhaps tomorrow?" Carol responded.

*Bet he says no. He's such a bozo.*

"Since we are on first names now, may I call you Carol? I would be happy if you called me Alex," Mr. Arthur stated.

***You're on, Miss Fluffy Britches. Just watch and learn.***

"Oh, yes, certainly," Carol replied.

"Good. Carol, Bill, we have scheduled the demolition company to start work the day after tomorrow. I would be pleased to show you the building, but I fear such an inspection may be for naught."

"Alex, were you aware that the city's Historic Preservation Committee is scheduled to meet today to discuss possibly getting the Clubhouse placed on the historic register because it was designed by a famous local architect?" the mayor asked.

"No, Bill, I was not aware of that proposed meeting. When is it set for?"

"The committee meets at six this evening. I was told that your company was sent a notice of the meeting over two weeks ago," the mayor replied.

"I'm sorry, Bill, but apparently, the notice never reached my desk. I'll have to speak to my staff about that...however, I presume that you will be there, Carol?"

"Yes, I have been asked to appear and give a presentation. However, without having been inside the building, I cannot say much. I was hoping I could postpone the meeting, inspect and analyze the condition and suitability of the building for renovation, and then make my report. Your demolition schedule rather puts a crimp in that idea — unless you could reschedule the demolition?"

"Folks, time is money. I have held off moving on the demolition for several months now, awaiting some sort of decision. My company has offered to put up a substantial sum to assist the city in moving the building. To date, we have gotten no positive response from the city."

"Hmm. I understand from the newspaper articles that the City has been pursuing a source of matching funds, but the State is dragging its feet. Surely, your folks have been aware of that problem, Alex," Carol stated matter-of-factly.

"Well, yes. But we have not had any sort of official response," the man said, almost grimacing as he spoke. He quickly resumed a neutral expression and added, "Okay, tell you what, I will delay the demolition for another month – I have other stuff the demo crew can do in the meantime. Carol, come by our office – next to the hospital complex – tomorrow. I will have written and signed a permission letter for you to inspect the building. Will that work for you all?"

### *Ha, ha – I told you so.*

"Yes, it will, Alex. Thank you," Carol replied, standing. "Now, if you gentlemen will excuse me, I have to get to another appointment and then to the committee meeting. Alex, my assistant, Amilee Lopez, or I will be at your office bright and early tomorrow morning. Bill, will you be there tonight?"

"No, sorry, Carol. I have a tete-a-tete with the City Manager after this. My wife invited a bunch of folks over for a celebratory dinner right after that."

"Celebratory dinner?" Alex queried.

"Yes, we are just now celebrating my election as Mayor."

"Well, my congrats on that, Bill. I hope you enjoy the dinner. Carol, I guess I'll see you at six?"

"Hasta luego, Alex, Bill," and Carol, followed by Rogue, left the office.

# Chapter Eight

Lyle and Carol sat in their living room, each with a glass of wine. Lyle jumped up from his chair and paced back and forth in front of the dead fireplace. Rogue was curled up on the sofa next to Carol.

"Shit, I don't know what to think or which way to jump. The Dean got a call from someone – he can't or won't say who. He is worried but not helpful, and no one seems to have any idea where this crap is coming from or why. I can't get a straight answer from anyone, and Bill Sheridan is conveniently not in his office."

"Love, sit down, you're driving me nuts," Carol responded, sipping her wine. "When did Sheridan say he would come to Cruces?"

"Hmm, let's see – he said next week. It is next week. I wonder if he'll show?"

"Let's give him a chance. We don't know what's going on – as you so clearly stated – he may be able or willing to provide some answers."

"Yeah, you are right. Actually, I looked Bill Sheridan up on the internet – he's an investigative interface between TSA and the CIA. So, it appears both agencies are involved – or at least interested. Shit – what a mess. The Dean suggested that I may need to travel back to Morocco. Damn – I hope not."

"Well, love, we will have to wait this one out, I think. How's that student doing on the information search?"

"She's doing great. I had to give her some pointers, and she has connected with the county archivist. She should have her preliminary report ready by next week. I have suggested that she also contact the Institute of Historical Survey, the UNM museum, and the State via whatever online connections she can find. When she finishes this little exercise, she will be ready to start on her master's research."

"Wow, that's great. I get the information I want for the Hysterical Committee, she gets some money and experience, and you get a well-trained hysterical researcher. Win, win, win."

"In fact, the young woman did say something about thanking you - but that seems to have slipped my feeble mind, what with all the other excitement."

"Ah yes — well, noted and forgiven — at least this time," Carol playfully chided, leaning over to kiss and nip her husband on the neck.

"Hey, go easy there, lover. The evening is young, and we haven't had supper yet."

Carol laughed and sipped her wine. Lyle leaned back in his recliner and pretended to doze off.

### *Someone's at the door.*

The doorbell and Carol's phone chimed. Carol looked at her phone. The man pictured at the door was none other than Bill Spencer.

"Speak of the devil, Lyle, and who should be at our door with his pitchfork, tail, and all?"

"You can't possibly mean Bill Spencer?"

"Ah, but that is exactly who I mean."

The doorbell and Carol's phone chimed again. "Come in, Bill, door's unlocked," Carol said.

The door opened and then closed. "Okay, I give. Where are you?" came from the vestibule.

"Through the doorway to your left. We are in the living room getting soused," Lyle responded.

Spencer appeared in the living room doorway, looked at Lyle and Carol, and said, "Where's my wine?" as he walked in and sat across from Lyle.

Carol stood up and offered her hand, which Bill shook. He looked at Lyle but didn't offer his hand.

"What's your poison, Bill?" Lyle asked. "We have Malbec, Cabet, and Merlot."

"Merlot sounds wonderful. It's been a long day, and I'm more than ready for some relaxation."

Carol headed for the kitchen. Lyle sat back up in his recliner and looked hard at Bill Spencer.

"Bill, I know you would like to small-talk, but I have also had a bad day. What the hell is going on with this manuscript crap?"

"I know you had a bad day, Lyle. I spoke to your Dean this morning after you were there. I think I have satisfied him that you are not an international manuscript thief."

"That's fine, and thank you. What about the CIA-looking folks and the two Arab men following Carol and me?"

"Lyle, those folks are all from the Moroccan consulate. They still think you have, or at least know, where the manuscript is. The problem you face, and one that the government faces diplomatically, is that the person who was supposed to get the manuscript swears he never got it. The other person from the team that you said handed over the manuscript has disappeared. We cannot get a statement from him. Interpol is looking for him, but so far, no leads."

"So," Carol began, handing Bill a glass of wine, "you need a witness that will support Lyle's statement and refute the Moroccan guy. Is that right?"

"Thank you, Carol. Yes, that is where we are. The CIA thinks that the Moroccan and the missing archaic manuscript expert are in cahoots. The CIA believes the plan is to peddle the manuscript on the black market or extort — blackmail — the Moroccan government to get it back. They seem to have complete faith in their man's testimony. Hence, Lyle must be the thief."

"Bill, I believe there is a reliable witness to Lyle handing over the manuscript. However, getting her to make a statement and getting Morocco to believe her could be a bit of a tango."

"Hmm, who would that be?" Bill responded, sipping his wine. "Hey, this is really good vino. Is it a New Mexico product?"

Lyle smiled and responded, "Yep, it's from a local winery. They do a great Cabernet, too."

Carol sipped from her own glass, looked at the fireplace momentarily, and responded, "Bill, an old woman helped us locate the manuscript in the mosque's wall. As with most of her class of folks, she was apparently figuratively invisible to the government and the other guy."

"Wow, you are right, Carol. There has been no mention of any old women present when Lyle handed the manuscripts over. Do you know how we might contact her?"

"Therein lies the problem. You see, the old woman is a seer — a witch in the eyes of most Moroccans. She is one of the invisible people that make the country run. She has a shop in one of the souks and does fortune-telling. I wandered into her shop one day, and for some reason, we struck it off nearly immediately. It was her vision that located the manuscripts. She was there when we found it, and she was there when it got handed over."

*You think Aliyah will cooperate?*

**Maybe. I think she trusts us.**

"So, you are telling me that you, a Ph.D. Engineer, and Lyle, a Ph.D. Historian, believe in those folk tales?"

It was Lyle that spoke in response. "I am telling you that the old woman went into a trance, and when she woke up, she led us directly to the manuscript. It was still buried in the wall, and I had to do a bit of archaeology to get it out, but it was right where she said it would be. You may believe or not as you see fit, Bill, but we can both testify to what occurred. The why's and how's will remain unknown, I think, forever."

Bill Spencer looked at Lyle and Carol and shook his head. "Okay, I will accept you at your word. How do we find and get a statement from the woman?"

It was Lyle that spoke in response. "I think the old lady trusts me. I will go back to Marrakech, locate her, and try to get her to make a statement. Carol needs to stay here. Her company just got a couple of lucrative contracts that require her presence. The Dean already said he would cover my classes to allow me to return to Morocco if necessary."

*Do you think she really trusts Lyle?*

***I think we will have to take that chance, my furry familiar.***

*As I recall, Aliyah's skinny black tom liked Lyle – so it'll probably be okay.*

***You're right. Aliyah tends to like and trust anyone that her familiar ankle rubs and he did like Lyle's ankles.***

"Lyle, I have orders from headquarters to accompany you to Marrakech, and I have a diplomatic passport for you, as well as flights on government aircraft. My bosses at the CIA want this sorted, quietly and quickly, so I'm extremely pleased that you have made this decision without coercion. Now, how about we do dinner somewhere nice – my treat – perhaps that winery that makes the delicious Merlot?"

Lyle and Carol looked at one another, smiled, shrugged their shoulders, and stood up.

"You're on, Bill. I'll make arrangements with the department chair and the Dean tomorrow. I can be on my way in two days. Will that work for you and your fearless leaders? You'd best have a really good expense account. They have a really great prime rib at the winery. And I know all the expensive places in Marrakech."

*The winery, humpf — you'd better put down some of that special cat food before you leave.*

**How about I bring a kitty bag home with some prime rib in it?**

*His expense account? Better be some of their grilled halibut.*

**Grilled halibut, it is.**

Carol chuckled as she took the empty glasses to the kitchen. Bill Spencer gave her a quizzical look but said nothing.

# Chapter Nine

When Carol pulled up to the house, the Albuquerque engineers' truck was already there.

*Hmm, early birds get the job.*

Carol walked up to the gate and noticed the engineer and George Percival kneeling at the corner of the house, animatedly talking. She stood for a moment, listening, then unlatched the gate and walked into the yard. At the sound of the gate opening, George and the engineer ceased their discussion to look up.

"Hello, Carol. Nice to see you again," the engineer said as he stood up and extended his hand.

George Percival also stood, "Hi, Dr. Montgomery. Your engineer got here a bit early. We were discussing what he sees as needing to be done."

"Jose, George, hello. It's nice to see you again, Jose. How's business?"

"Busier than the proverbial cat on a tin roof, Carol. Thank you for bringing us back down for this one."

"So, what have you decided regarding the corner, Jose?"

"Carol, nothing has changed much since the last time I was here. A bit more settling, but it looks like not watering this flower bed has pretty well stopped the subsidence. I think one of our standard hydraulic jacks, just in from the corner, will do the job. We haven't looked at the fireplace yet."

"Okay. George, can we go inside and let Jose take a look?"

"Yes, of course. Let's do it."

"Where's your cat, Carol?" Jose asked. "Surely she's not gone."

"No, she's fine. Sleeping off a big piece of fish from dinner last night. We went with a friend to the winery on Avenida de Mesilla. The guy owed us one, so we got Rogue a grilled halibut steak."

"Lucky cat. The winery grills the best halibut anywhere I've eaten," Jose responded. "Okay, let's go look at the fireplace."

George gave Carol and Jose a sidelong look, then led them into the house.

Jose stood in front of the fireplace and looked carefully at the brickwork. He got onto his knees and closely examined the hearth. Jose then ran his hand up inside the fireplace below the mantle. When he finished, he stood up, dusted his hand on his pants, stepped back a short way, and gazed long and hard at the fireplace.

"Yes, Carol, I agree the fireplace needs to be stabilized. It won't come crashing down tomorrow, but it is settling. We can lift the hearth and get under the floor here. When we get there, I think we can put some standard floor jacks under the joists. That will stabilize the fireplace and the rest of the room. With that done and the corner stabilized, the house and fireplace should have another hundred years."

George spoke up, "About the cost? How much more than your preliminary estimate do you think it will cost?"

"Mr. Percival, I need to calculate that, but it should not double the original estimate. I would say, roughly not more than twelve hundred dollars more," Jose replied.

"When can you start?" Carol asked. "I need to be involved because I promised the Historic Protection Committee that I would supervise the work. They would be happier if they had to approve the permit, but I am having one of Lyle's grad students do a historical records search. I'll give the committee the report."

"That's a good idea, Carol. I know those folks can be a real pain – at least the ones in Albuquerque can."

"And what will that supervision cost?" George asked.

"Nothing above my original proposal to you," Carol replied, "provided they don't hit any snags that call for my participation beyond riding herd on the project."

"And what might those snags be, Dr. Montgomery?"

"I don't know, Mr. Percival. I only mention the possibility because, as we all know, if anything can go wrong, it will. I truly don't anticipate anything, however."

"Very well, Mr. Fierro, Dr. Montgomery, please do get started. As soon as I receive the final contract, I will ante up the requested half of the estimate. Now, I am expecting a business associate, so I must show you the door."

"Thank you, Mr. Percival. I will have the contract to you by noon tomorrow at the latest. Jose, let's meet at the coffee shop across from NMSU and thrash out the final costs."

"Great, Carol. See you at the coffee shop in about thirty minutes. Mr. Percival, thank you, and I'll see you again soon."

Carol drove by her office and picked up Rogue on her way to the coffee shop. Ami was buried in bookkeeping and shrugged off the offer of coffee and a bagel. Rogue was ecstatic at the prospect.

*Everything's coming up, meeces, to misquote the song. Grilled halibut, then a cup of half-and-half at the coffee shop.*

**Don't get your hopes up too high, my familiar. This, too, may pass.**

Carol, with Rogue at her heels, walked into the coffee shop and spotted Jose at a table near the back. She waved, put in her order at the register, and, with Rogue at her heels, walked back to the table.

"Hi, Rogue," Jose said as Carol sat down, and Rogue jumped up on the third chair.

"Meow," Rogue replied.

"Carol, I don't like that Percival guy. He is way too formal and quick to say bye."

"You and Ami have the same sense of him. I tend to agree, but I think a lot of it is his cultural background. I gather from his accent that English may be his second language, with Arabic as his first. You noticed there was no sign of a woman around the house when we entered. Based on my recent adventures in Morocco, I believe that is a common situation in more or less traditional Muslim households. The women stay out of sight of strangers, especially male strangers."

"I think I heard something about you being sent to Morocco to help with the earthquake damage. It was a big adventure, was it?"

"Neat place, Marrakech, but I sure don't envy them rebuilding some of those ancient, historical buildings. Next time you're down here, I'll regale you with tall tales and other lies."

"So, anyway, you think he's honest?"

"I have done a little background checking on him and his company. As far as I can tell, he is completely straight-arrow. A very formal arrow, though, I must say," Carol said with a smile and chuckle.

"Okay, I trust your judgment, my friend. Here is my best guestimate of costs," Jose said, handing Carol a piece of his company's letterhead. "I made good use of the time waiting for you and of my phone. My estimator crunched the numbers for me as I guzzled this good coffee. I'll send you a formal proposal when I get back to Albuquerque."

"Thank you, Jose. The numbers look good. That's pretty much what I suspected and very close to my informal estimate. How's your esposa and hijo?"

"They are muy bueno, Carol, thanks for asking. The boy's getting close to graduating from high school and says he wants to be an engineer, like his old man. We'll see. He's sharp as a tack and a math whiz, but, damn, he plays a mean guitar."

"I understand that. Our young man is nearly done with his Bachelor's in psychology. He's applying to grad school in California – UCLA, I think, he said. Apparently, neither history nor engineering holds any attraction for him. So it goes."

"How's Lyle doing? I understand that he got his full professorship, and you guys spent some time in D.C. for his Sabbatical. Back at the grind, is he?"

"Actually, he's getting ready to go back to Marrakech tomorrow. Some sort of a lash up on some work he did for their government while we were there."

"Oh, no major problemas, I hope."

"I don't think so. He's got a government escort, a guy he met while he was on Sabbatical at Howard University, and a diplomatic passport. I'm sure he'll be back here in a week or less."

"Sounds interesting," Jose looked at his watch. "Oh shite, Carol. I have to run. I have a meeting at one of the engineering companies across town. They have a project that sounds like it will require lots of our piers."

"See you in a few days then, Jose. Drive carefully going home."

"Hasta luego, Carol," Jose said as he stood up and left.

*He's a nice person, Carol. Mmm, mmm, that half-and-half was good. Any chance of a refill?*

# Chapter Ten

Carol knocked and walked into Lyle's university office, Rogue at her heels. Lyle was at his desk with a young woman across from him, both concentrating on a document on Lyle's desk. Lyle looked up and stood as soon as he noticed Carol.

"Hey, hello. Come in and pull up a chair. Phyllis and I were just reviewing the steps she should try to follow to do the search on your property. Oh, Phyllis, this is my wife, Dr. Montgomery. Carol, this is Phyllis Crowne. Phyllis hails from Melbourne, and I'm still trying to understand what brought her here."

Phyllis stood and offered her hand to Carol. Carol reached out and shook Phyllis's hand -  a slight tingle occurred as she did so. Phyllis looked slightly startled.

"Phyllis, how nice to meet you. Sorry for the static nip; my cat does that to some of these microfiber blouses. This is Rogue; she's my companion and sometimes the bane of my existence."

*Bane, bah! Cat static, double bah! She's fairly glowing with Wiccan power.*

***You are right, Rogue, but I don't sense that she knows that. So, let's let it ride for now. We'll see what transpires as we work with her.***

"Dr. Montgomery, yes - great to meet you. Cats, balloons, and static – I'm familiar with that."

"All right, Lyle, what do I need to do to coordinate with Phyllis while you are out of town?" Carol asked as she pulled up a chair and sat down next to the desk. Rogue jumped onto her lap, purring softly.

"Not really too much, Carol. I have cleared it with the department chair, so you will have access to Phyllis without any impediments. Phyllis has agreed to work directly with you and to report to you as she moves forward in her search. The list we were just perusing has the names, emails, and phone numbers of the woman at the courthouse who is in charge of the files, as well as the person at the Historical Research Institute who is responsible for the files there. The list includes web access for UNM's system. I can't think of any additional points of access Phyllis may need."

"How about if Phyllis stumbles onto some source that you haven't covered?" Carol responded.

"The department chair is prepared to provide assistance there, as needed."

"Phyllis, do you have any questions for me? I know it's early, and you likely will have as you go forward."

Phyllis looked at the list, put her hands together and rotated her thumbs for a moment in thought, then replied, "No, ma'am, I don't think so. May I come by your office and bug you if I need to or want to update you?"

"For sure, Phyllis. Just be sure to give me a call ahead of time if you can. I'm often out with clients or at meetings."

"Understood, Dr. Montgomery. This should be rather fun, and I'm thinking it may provide the basis for my thesis."

Lyle Parnassus, Bill Spencer, and several others walked up the boarding ladder and found seats in the executive jet parked near the general aviation portion of the El Paso airport. Bill and Lyle sat near the door toward the rear of the plane. Lyle stowed his briefcase above the seat, sat down, and scanned the other passengers. He stopped his scan when he noticed two people in gray suits, one with a hijab, sitting near the front of the cabin. Lyle quickly retrieved his briefcase from overhead and pulled out a small notepad.

Sitting back down, he took a pen out of his shirt pocket and jotted a note in the notepad, which he handed to Bill.

> *Bill, what do you know about the couple up in row three on the other side of the cabin?*

Bill read the note, took out his own pen to write below Lyle's note, and handed the pad back to Lyle.

> *Fakira Ouhabi and Bakkar Choukri, both native Moroccan. Bakkar, according to his surname, is of Amazigh heritage, with familial connections to Mohammed. They are both CIA agents attached to the Moroccan Embassy in Rabat.*

Lyle responded and returned the paper.

> *I think they are the couple that was bird-dogging Carol. How about the two rather scruffy-looking dudes behind them?*

Bill read Lyle's question, then wrote his response and handed the note to Lyle.

> *Those two work for the Moroccan government. I don't know their names.*

Lyle responded.

> *They look like the pair that were bird-dogging me.*

Bill wrote back.

> *I believe that, with you returning to Marrakech, the heelers have been called off.*

*Fakira and Bakkar have been assigned to accompany us to act as translators and, of course, watchers. I don't know about the other two, except that they seem to be going home with us.*

*See the two guys sitting in Aisle five? They are your security detail. When we are airborne, I will give you a vest to put on under your clothes — I already have mine on. There are those in Morocco who may want to eliminate you, and likely me, too.*

*Both sides of the fence. The hard-core fundamentalist Islamists consider losing the manuscripts to be an insult to Mohammed, and whoever stole the manuscripts would rather not get caught.*

Lyle looked at Bill's last scribble, looked at Bill, then scribbled,

*Shit, my friend. Now, you tell me that my life may be in danger. Thanks loads.*

Bill laughed softly and responded.

*Lyle, you would not have agreed to do this if I had been straight with you. Getting this resolved and hopefully finding and retrieving the manuscripts is super important to our government. I just got an email from a friend in Vienna. Interpol thinks they have a lead on the thieves.*

Lyle stared at the overhead panel and said nothing as the pilot announced their impending take-off. The small jet pulled onto the taxiway, rolled  onto the runway, and accelerated, lifting off the runway in about half the distance of a commercial jet. Lyle remained still, pressed back in his seat by the acceleration, and pondered the future. When the seatbelt sign turned off, he turned to Bill and said, rather flatly, "Where's my life vest?"

Bill signaled Lyle to stand in the aisle, stood up, opened the overhead bin across the aisle, and removed a package. Lyle accepted the package and walked back to the restroom. A few minutes later, he returned to his seat, looking a bit more robust in the chest than earlier.

"Lyle, I really am sorry we had to do things this way. I hope neither of us needs the vest, and I truly hope that things go smoothly in Marrakech," Bill said as Lyle sat down.

"Bill, I fully understand. When I came home from Nam at eighteen, I thought I was through being chronically afraid for my life. Clearly, I was wrong. Being a stuffy history professor also seems to come with long stretches of boredom punctuated by moments of absolute terror. I just wish I had been able to up my life insurance policy before we left."

Bill Spencer looked at his companion and smiled slightly, "Actually, the government took care of that for you."

Lyle looked over at Bill, stared for a moment, then laughed uproariously. "Mi amigo, are you sure we aren't in a comedic dream?"

*Hi Love –*

*Here we are in beeyootiful downtown Madrid. It's been an interesting flight so far. It's faster than the commercials, but there are lots more stops for fuel. We have a short layover here to change crews, then off again. The next stop is Rabat, and then we drive to Marrakech.*

*I met the couple that were tailing you. Nice folks, actually. They work for the CIA from the U.S. Embassy in Morocco. The pair that were following me were also on the plane. They don't speak any English, as far as I can tell, and apparently work for the Moroccan government. Both pairs know one another but were sent to the States independently. The Moroccan government pair apparently begged a ride home after they figured out that I was going back to Morocco. All of those spooks seem to know one another.*

*Okay, new crew just went on board. Need to use the little boys' room, then back on the plane. Take care.*

*- Lyle*

# Chapter Eleven

Carol read Lyle's email and responded.

*Hi Lyle –*

*I guess you will be in Rabat when you get this email. Phyllis got me her preliminary report yesterday. She verified the age of the house and the ownership chain. She is still digging for some information about the original owner and builder. I have enough, however, for the Hysterical Committee. With any luck, the guys should be able to start the corner stabilization in a day or two. The fireplace and subfloor stuff will take a little longer, and they won't begin that work until the corner is done.*

*Hope all is well and you return home soon. I am lonely as hell, but Rogue keeps the bed warm.*

*Love ya,*

*- Carol*

⌂ ⌂ ⌂

Carol stopped in front of the house and sat for a moment, watching the workmen digging at the corner. The hydraulic pier was lying on the ground nearby. *Looks like they are close to having that corner done. Time to go inside and see if they've started on the fireplace.* Carol climbed out of her truck, walked through the gate, and rang the doorbell.

"Dr. Montgomery, please do come in," the woman said. "My husband is away right now. What can I do for you?"

"Hello, Mrs. Percival. I stopped by to check on how the work was proceeding on the corner and the fireplace. I take it the stabilization crew have not yet started on the fireplace."

"Yes, that is true. My husband asked them to delay doing the inside work until he returned from his trip, which should be the day after tomorrow. It appears that the men are nearly done with the corner, however."

"You are correct. I believe that the stabilization crew will probably finish there today. My husband's graduate student has been doing a historical background search, and she has found some interesting information about the original builder. I'll have to provide you and your husband with a copy of the final report."

"That would be wonderful, Dr. Montgomery. My husband is quite the historical building buff. That's the main reason we purchased this house. We have been told that it was built around 1910 by a local attorney who subsequently returned to Texas."

"Yes, I believe that is fundamentally correct. The interesting part, I think, has to do with the builder's history. We'll see that story when Miss Crowne submits her final report."

"May I offer you a cup of tea, Dr. Montgomery?"

"Why yes, that would be nice."

Carol sat down in the living room as Mrs. Percival brought steaming cups of tea.

"Dr. Montgomery, may I ask you a question about the history of this house?"

"Of course, but I may or may not have an answer."

"Well, I do not believe in ghosts," Mrs. Percival began.

"Nor do I," Carol interjected. "But I do maintain an open mind with regard to some of the things that happen in the world."

"Well then, my ten-year-old daughter believes that she has seen one in this house."

"Let me guess, a man in a gray duster and hat is just standing near the fireplace in the dining room."

"Yes. Unsettling, to say the least. How did you know that?"

"I heard about the gray man from the prior owners when we were originally looking at the corner settling."

"Hmm. I don't know how to respond to my daughter. She is not inclined to exaggerate and has never reported anything like that to me in the past."

"Mrs. Percival, I'm not quite sure how to respond either. The previous owner's daughter maintained that she regularly saw what she called 'the gray man'. I have not seen anything like that, but I have spent very little time inside the house and none at night when the gray man is purported to appear. Which is typical ghost behavior, according to believers."

"Should I believe what my daughter says or perhaps seek counseling for her?"

"For now, I would advise doing nothing. If your daughter reports seeing the gray man again, then you might want to think about an exorcism of the house. That is what the previous owners did and, apparently, the daughter stopped seeing the supposed ghost."

"Thank you, Dr. Montgomery. If push comes to shove, I will consult with our Imam. A Christian exorcism would not fit in our beliefs, but the Imam might offer a substitute. Meanwhile, I will remain silent. My husband would be very likely to go off the deep end and take us all to counseling if he heard the story."

"I will remember that and say nothing — ah, this is wonderful tea. However, I must be going. My assistant is no doubt pacing with anxiety since I have an appointment at City Hall."

"I understand. Thank you, and stop by any time you would like tea and a chat."

"Thank you," Carol said and put her empty cup on the coffee table, stood, nodded to Mrs. Percival, and left. Just as she got to her truck, her phone played its usual call tune. She slid in and answered the call.

"Hi Ami, what's up?"

"Carol, I got a call from Phyllis Crowne today. She wants to meet at the office this afternoon. She indicated that it was important."

"Okay, Ami. I'm on my way back to the office. See you in a few minutes. Did Phyllis give you any clues about what she needs to talk about?"

"Not really. Only that it had to do with past ownership of the Hadley place."

"On my way, Watson. Just had tea, but will probably need a large mug of coffee."

⌂ ⌂ ⌂

"Phyllis, hello. Come on in. This is my assistant, Amilee Lopez — Ami. We just made coffee. Can I interest you in a cup? Or perhaps tea?"

"Yes, thank you, Dr. Montgomery. Coffee would be great."

"Ami, please get Ms. Crowne a mug of coffee. Phyllis, park yourself on the couch and tell me what's going on."

Phyllis Crowne sat on the couch, and Rogue jumped up on her lap.

"Rogue, don't be pestering Phyllis," Carol said.

"It's okay, Dr. Montgomery. I like cats."

Rogue purred loudly and kneaded Phyllis's leg.

*Wow, she is strong in the force, as Yoda would say.*

**Yes, I can feel it clear over here. Let's hear what she has to say.**

"Well, Dr. Montgomery, I was just at the Historical Research Institute, going through some stuff they have for the house on Hadley. I came across a will and a sort of diary written by the original owner."

"Please, call me Carol. So, what did you find in those documents?"

Ami walked in and handed Carol and Phyllis mugs of coffee, then sat at her desk with her own mug.

"Thank you, Ami," Carol said as she sipped the fresh brew. "This is good. New brand?"

"Thank you, Mrs. Lopez. Wow, this is good," Phyllis said as she sipped from the mug and set it on the coffee table.

"Just Ami, please. Yes, Milagro has a new shipment of beans, and this is their new dark roast, Carol."

"We'll have to buy this one again. Phyllis, please go ahead," Carol responded.

"Well, the short answer is that there may be a baby buried under the fireplace."

"Oh my gosh," Ami snorted. "Are you sure?"

"Well, according to the diary, the original owner and his wife buried their firstborn near the small adobe that they had built. They were forced out of the adobe when someone purchased the property and decided to subdivide it. The couple traveled up the Camino to Santa Fe thereafter. The man became an attorney, and they subsequently were very successful. They returned to Las Cruces and purchased the lot in the subdivision where their home had been. Where they buried their child."

"Hmm, that area was not subdivided until about 1910. When did they originally live there? Did the diary say?" Carol asked.

"Based on what I found in the property tax records, the person who purchased the property never subdivided it, and for some time, the land remained vacant or may have had a goat farm on it. The property changed hands several times and then was subdivided. I can't tell for sure from the diary, but the original house owner and builder must have bought the lot not long after it was subdivided. Anyway, the man, now a successful attorney, built the house over the child's grave. Specifically, he placed the fireplace over the burial spot."

"Wow, now that's a story," Ami exclaimed.

"Phyllis, based on what you have told us, we need to halt the renovation of the fireplace."

"Yes, that is why I wanted to talk to you. According to the will I found, there is a family plot in the Masonic Cemetery. The child's remains should be re-interred there."

"Hmm, I wonder why they never re-interred the child?" Carol asked.

"I think that they may have intended to, but then life got in the way," Phyllis replied.

"Phyllis, in your search, have you found anything about a ghost in the house?" Carol asked. "The previous owners and the current owners have told me of what appears to be a man in a gray duster and hat occupying the house and hanging out around the fireplace."

"As a matter of fact, I did find a newspaper clipping from some time after the attorney's passing. Someone reported such a gray man, and it got into the local newspaper. There were no real details, just a short article about local ghost stories."

"Hmm – Okay, I need to call Jose and let him know. The owner has asked that the workmen not come into the house because he's not there. He should be back in town tomorrow, according to his wife. I also need to notify the city and the police that a child may be buried there. This is going to complicate the work, but there's not much else we can do. If we did nothing and they found the remains while trying to get under the house, all hell would break loose."

"Carol, how about next of kin? If the child is to be reinterred in a family plot, the family will need to know and give their permission," Ami said.

"That's a good point, Ami. Thank you. Phyllis, have you seen anything in the papers you found that points to next of kin?"

"No, I haven't."

"Carol, let me check with the Masonic Cemetery folks. They should have records that would identify the family," Ami offered.

"Thank you again, Ami. Please do that."

# Chapter Twelve

s Lyle, Bill, and their security started down the jet's loading stairs, a shot rang out. One of the security men tumbled down the stairs. Bill quickly grabbed Lyle and pulled him back into the aircraft. The remaining security man knelt, pistol drawn, and looked across the tarmac. A person could be seen running away from the fence with what looked like a rifle in their hands. He took aim and fired two rounds at the running figure, who stumbled and fell, but managed to regain footing and continued into the buildings along the airport's runways and loading area. The security person who had fallen down the stairs stood up and indicated that he was alright. Bill slowly stood and let Lyle up.

"What the hell? How can I prove my innocence if I'm dead?" Lyle said, wiping his hands on his pants.

"I strongly suspect that's exactly what someone has in mind, Lyle," Bill responded. "Someone wants you to be the thief."

The security person that had fired at the assailant turned around and said, "Dr. Parnassus, Mr. Spencer, are you okay?"

"Yes, we are fine but shaken up," Bill replied.

"I think I have a bruise on my knee," Lyle said, chuckling. "Bill, you are a wonderful defender, but your tactic nearly squashed me."

"Sorry, Lyle. That's what they train us to do in spook school."

"C'mon down, you guys. Let's get gone before they decide to try again," the one on the tarmac shouted.

The three men hurried down the stairs and were hustled into a waiting car.

A man with binoculars looked out over the airport runway and mumbled in Arabic, as he stood atop a minaret of the Mohammed VI Mosque, "The fools. I told them to wait. Now, the Americans are on alert."

The car drove rapidly out of the airport via a security gate. The road ran along the coast and then turned along what amounted to embassy row, passing the Swiss Embassy and several others before reaching the U.S. Embassy. The two security guards hopped out of the limousine first and quickly scanned the area before signaling to Bill Spencer and Lyle Parnassus to leave the car. The men were swiftly hustled into the embassy building and shown to an office well away from the extensive glass front of the building.

⌂ ⌂ ⌂

Carol's phone played a riff from "I Did It My Way," her usual ringtone. Carol excused herself from the meeting with the Mayor and Chief of Police and stepped into the hall.

"Carol, sorry to interrupt your meeting, but I just got a call from the History Department at NMSU. A package just arrived, addressed to Lyle with a Brussels postmark, but no return address. Should I go by and get it?" Ami asked.

"Yes, please do. I should be finished with this chin-wag about the possible burial at the house on Hadley in about ten minutes. I'll be back in the office in less than a half hour."

"Very good. See you then."

Carol walked back into the mayor's office and closed the door. "Mayor, Chief, have we got a plan for how to handle this possible burial thing? I need to get back to my office. A package from Europe has come for my husband. I suspect it has something to do with the reason he's back in Morocco."

"Carol, the Chief, and I agree that the burial is not a police or a city matter but falls into the bailiwick of the archaeology folks at NMSU," the mayor said.

"Yes. I will contact the head of the Anthropology Department as soon as I get back to my office," the police chief said. "I will request that they follow up with your husband's graduate student and the Historical Research Institute to develop a plan to determine if there is a burial and then a way to exhume it with minimal problems for the homeowners. There may need to be a forensic examination of the remains. If an archaeologist testifies that it is more than 100 years old, I believe the regulations and law will be satisfied."

"That's wonderful, gentlemen. We are moving forward," Carol replied. "Now I need to get my derriere back to my office."

⌂ ⌂ ⌂

"Carol," Ami said as Carol walked into the office, "The school would not release the package to me. The lady in the office said that the chairman was holding it, and it was only to be released to Lyle or to you."

"Well, crap. Okay, I'll go get it. Then, I need to email Lyle and let him know about it. I suspect that he'll want me to forward it to him."

"Also, George Percival called. He wants an explanation of what is holding up the work on the house. I told him I would have you return his call."

"Double crap. I'll call Mr. Percival, then head for NMSU. Wait, I can call him while I am driving. I'll just use my new hands-free."

"That sounds like an idea – but do be careful, boss. You know how dangerous driving and talking on the phone are."

*Can I come? I've been stuck sitting here listening to your head all day. Please, please.*

**All right, brat cat. Let's go.**

"Ami, I'm taking her fuzziness with me. I'll be careful. I have used hands-free before, just not recently."

"Okay, I'll see you in a while unless you get back after closing time. I have to get home. I promised Anthony I'd watch LeeAnn so he and Trish could go to a movie."

"Got it. I should be back by quitting time. If you leave before I get back, my best to the kids and give LeeAnn a hug for me."

Carol selected the number for George Percival on her cell phone. "Hello, Mr. Percival. I'm driving and using my hands-free device. — The delay you are concerned about is because my researcher found an old diary that suggests that there may be a baby buried under your fireplace. Because we don't want you or our workers to have to deal with a one-hundred-year-old corpse, the city and the police department are arranging for an archaeologist from the university to dig out the area under the fireplace. No, sir. There will be no charge to you for the archaeological work. If there is a baby under the fireplace, the body will be reinterred in a family plot at the Masonic cemetery. I can come by tomorrow, Mr. Percival. Right now, I have an errand to take care of for my husband, who is out of town. Okay, very good. I will see you tomorrow afternoon. Yes, thank you. Take care, and don't worry, the person that will be doing the digging is very professional and has done similar things previously."

Carol clicked off her phone and pulled into a parking space near Breland Hall. Inside, she climbed the stairs to the history department's office on the second floor and walked into the office.

The secretary greeted her, "Dr. Montgomery, hello. Dr. Sampson has your husband's package. Go right in; he's expecting you."

"Charles, how are you," Carol said as she walked into the office. "Do you have any idea what's in the package?"

"Hello, Carol. Not a glimmer, but I suspect it has something to do with why Lyle's in Morocco again. It does not have a return address, but it is postmarked from Brussels."

"Hmm, that may or may not suggest anything positive. Well, here I am, so I guess the package is now mine to sort out."

"Indeed. Weird stuff going on. I hope this points to Lyle getting back sooner rather than later. I had to assign his classes to a part-timer. She's good but has never done a class in Southwestern Native American history before."

"Yes, inconvenient at a minimum. If she hasn't already thought of it, I think one of Lyle's grad students has some familiarity and perhaps can help her."

"I'm not sure, but I will suggest that to her. Here's the package. I put it inside a Ziplock bag, just in case anyone might need to dust it for prints or DNA. However, it's probably gone through so many hands by now that anything of value is blitzed."

"Thank you, Charles," Carol responded as she accepted the plastic bag. "Good thinking. I had actually not thought about that. I'll use my leftover COVID gloves when I open it – if I open it. I need to email Lyle and see what, if anything, he wants me to do with it."

"Say hi and hurry home for me, please. We miss Lyle's witticisms in staff meetings."

"Will do. How's planning going for the grad student luncheon this semester?"

"Very well, Carol. We all hope Lyle is back in time to participate."

"Me too," she waved goodbye and walked out the door.

"Bye, Dr. Montgomery. Best to Dr. Parnassus when you contact him," the secretary said as Carol made her way out the door, and waved from over her shoulder as she turned down the hall toward the stairs. When she got to her truck, she sent Lyle an email.

*Lyle – got the package from Brussels. It may be a Xerox of the original manuscript. It's too heavy to be old parchment. Rogue and I are going to give it a going-over this evening. I'll let you know what we find if anything. Take care, my love. Charles sends his greetings and a desire for you to get back ASAP. His secretary sends her greetings.*

*- Carol*

The office was empty as Carol returned, Ami having gone home, and Rogue jumped onto her lap, purring. With a pair of plastic gloves on her hands, she pulled the package out of the bag, noting the Brussels postmark and lack of any return address. Rogue leapt onto the desk and sniffed the package from end to end.

***Well, my familiar, what do you make of this package?***

*It vibrates with someone's identity. We need to work it over.*

***I agree. Let's move over to the house, sit in front of the fireplace, and find out who is attached to this package.***

Carol stood up, and Rogue landed on the floor. Both made their way out of the office, across the yard, and into the house. She left the package on the coffee table in front of the fireplace, walked to her closet bookshelf, and removed a thick, old book. Returning with the book, she sat on the couch as Rogue jumped up beside her.

***Rogue, I haven't done one of these spells for years. I'm going to need to read how to do it to make sure I haven't forgotten anything. Wouldn't want to incinerate the package or turn it into a butterfly.***

*Good idea, my witch. I'll sit here and listen to your mind as you read. Maybe a snack would be in order. We wouldn't want to start important stuff on an empty stomach.*

***Do you ever not think about food? Okay, let me fetch a bit of that halibut for you and a cookie for me. How does that sound?***

*I couldn't have asked for better. Are you sure a cookie is enough for you?*

***Well, maybe a bagel and cream cheese would be better.***

*How about some of the cheese instead of halibut for me? I haven't had cream cheese forever.*

***Spoiled brat cat – Okay – consider it done.***

The woman left her place on the couch and walked to the kitchen. Rogue remained loafing on the cushions and could hear the refrigerator open, as well as the small noises associated with toasting a bagel and spreading the cream cheese. Carol stepped back into the room and placed a prepared bagel on the coffee table, along with a small saucer of cream cheese. Carol began munching as she read through the big book, while Rogue chomped the contents of the saucer

After wiping her fingers and lips on a paper towel, Carol closed the book and looked at the package lying on the table. Rogue licked the last of the cream cheese from the plate and cocked her head toward Carol.

*Well, my witch, are you ready?*

***Yes, my familiar, I am. Let's begin.***

⌂ ⌂ ⌂

Carol shook her head slightly, stared at the ceiling for a moment, then placed the package back in the Ziplock bag. She picked her phone up from the coffee table, selected email, and sent her husband a note.

> *Lyle – Rogue and I have examined the package very carefully. I believe that we can specify the identity of the person who sent it. I presume they are the thief. A short, swarthy individual with a big mustache. I think he was there when you handed the manuscript to the government guy. Aliyah can probably identify him for you. If not, I can send a sketch – but you know what a lousy artist I am.*
>
> *Luv U,*
>
> *Carol*

The email bing-bong on Carol's phone sounded within a minute after she hit the send button.

> *Carol – Thank you. Sorry to be slow responding to your earlier email. We were en route from Rabat to Marrakech. By the way, we got shot at when we stepped off the plane. Seems that one of the Imams has written, but not announced, a Fatwa, an edict calling for me to be punished as the thief of an important Islamic text. The folks at the Embassy think the shooter was someone hired by the thieves to claim they were meeting the Fatwa but got ahead of themselves. I'm Okay. Aliyah has disappeared, as has the government dude that took the manuscript. However, I vaguely recall a guy with a big mustache. Please send me a sketch – even with your lack of artistic talent, I think it will help. My handlers say we should send the package, unopened, to Interpol in Brussels. I'll text you an address as soon as I can. Meanwhile, bag the package and don't handle it any more than necessary. Hopefully, Interpol will be able to trace where it was mailed from and may be able to get DNA or prints from it. We are staying in one of the nicer Riads in Marrakech. There are some benefits to being a spook for the government.*
>
> *Luv U 2,*
>
> *Lyle*

Carol responded to her husband's email as soon as she finished reading it.

> *Lyle – Gads, I'm glad you are okay. Did they catch the shooter? Your department chair had the foresight – insight? – to bag the package. Except when we evaluated it, and I was wearing plastic gloves, it has been in a Ziplock bag and unopened. I'll text you a sketch ASAP. I'll mail the bagged package as soon as I get an address from you. Oh, please be safe, my dear. I already miss you more than I can say. Rogue sends her positive thoughts, too.*
>
> *Oh, nearly forgot. The Interpol people may well find some DNA and print fragments from another person, perhaps the illegal antiquities dealer, on the package. My womanly instincts are pretty solid, I think. You might want to drop a hint to Interpol if they haven't already gotten it sorted. But, hey, they are professionals, que no?*
>
> *Luv,*
>
> *Carol*

# Chapter Thirteen

arol walked out of the post office and climbed into her truck. Rogue jumped up on her shoulder, purring, as the woman updated her. "The package has been mailed. I emailed Lyle a sketch of the guy we sussed on the package. Now, we hope Interpol will be efficient and catch the baddies. We have to go to Mr. Percival's place now. The university archaeologist is supposed to start work today, and Mr. Percival is understandably anxious."

*How about a stop at the coffee shop? I badly need a cup of half-and-half; that spell to see who sent the package wore me out.*

"Cat, that was yesterday. Okay, on the way home, then, I have to make sure all is going well with the fireplace excavation."

Carol parked behind the University vehicle in front of the house. A small group of people were standing on the front porch, talking among themselves.

"Rogue, stay here in the truck, please. Mr. Percival has no pets, and I suspect that a cat might upset his applecart."

*Okay, gotcha, boss. Don't be too long. I have goodies in my mind.*

The feline meowed softly and curled up on the driver's seat. Carol closed the truck door, walked up the steps, and greeted the older woman who appeared to be in charge of the group.

"Dr Montgomery, how good to see you," the woman responded. "Meet my digging crew."

Carol shook hands with each of the students, then spoke again to the leader, "Dr. Bonaparte, have you spoken to Mr. Percival yet?"

"Yes, he came out, and we chatted briefly. We are waiting for him to give us the go-ahead to start. I need to examine the fireplace before we do, so I hope he does not take too long to let us in."

"Alice, FYI, there is a story of a ghost – a man in a gray duster and hat – that is seen from time to time, usually in cold, windy winter weather, standing in front of the fireplace. Mr. Percival is not aware of the story, but his wife is because their daughter has seen the man in gray. Please say nothing to Mr. Percival about the story – it is FYI only – and your crew, of course."

"Folks, you heard Dr. Montgomery. Mum's the word. We'll talk more about it later, OK?"

George Percival opened the front door and stepped out onto the porch. "Dr. Montgomery, good morning. I'm glad you came by. Dr. Bonaparte, the dining room is clear. You and your students may get started. Dr. Montgomery, may we chat for a moment, please?"

"Thank you, Mr. Percival," Dr. Bonaparte said, then nodded. "Come on, troops, we have a lot of work to do and not a lot of time to do it," and she and the students walked into the house.

George and Carol stood aside as the students trooped in, the man closing the door behind them. He stepped to the edge of the porch to look up and down the street, then turned and spoke to Carol.

"Dr. Montgomery, we have heard some mumbling from the neighbors – well, actually, my daughter overheard some mumbling from a girl her age who lives down the street. It seems that some folks are making critical remarks about our being here and about my wife and daughter's hijabs. I know you have nothing to do with that. They are also, apparently, raising some questions about the baby in the fireplace and suggesting that we may have some evil influence. Is there anything that the city or someone can do to clarify that we inherited, so to speak, the burial?"

Percival's forehead was wrinkled into a frown, and he looked perplexed.

"Mr. Percival, I am so sad to hear that. I suppose one of the problems is that this is an old Hispanic family neighborhood that goes back to the early days of Las Cruces as a city. The gentrification of the neighborhood is not viewed positively by all of the residents, especially those whose families have been here for several generations. This is outside my area of expertise, but let me speak to the mayor. I think we can get a small article in the Sun-News and the Bulletin that explains the history of this house and why there may be a baby buried under the fireplace. Beyond that, I'm not sure what, if anything, we can do."

Percival sighed in apparent relief. "Thank you, Dr. Montgomery. I realize that you are limited in what you can do, and I appreciate the feelings of the neighbors. We had similar occurrences in my home village in Morocco when I was a young boy. Shall we go in and see how Dr. Bonaparte and her students are doing?"

"Yes, by all means. Did the folks get here and put up all of the protective stuff to keep the house clean? And Morocco, you say. That's interesting. My husband and I were just there doing some work for the Moroccan government, under U.S. sponsorship, to help with the post-quake damage and possible recovery of some of the old mosques and other historic structures."

"Yes, I had heard that you were there in your role as an adobe expert. What did you think of my homeland?"

"Morocco is a beautiful place, and the history is phenomenal."

"Yes, it is a lovely place. I sometimes miss it a great deal," Percival said, a note of fondness and nostalgia in his voice. "The protective stuff was taken care of yesterday. All we needed to do this morning was to move the dining room table into the living room. My wife, daughter, and I were able to do that easily. It's a small table."

"Very good. You should have asked for some help from the students."

"No, I prefer that we do those things ourselves, which protects my wife and daughter's privacy."

"I understand. Okay, let's see what's happening in the fireplace."

Carol and Mr. Percival walked into the dining room. Dr. Bonaparte was kneeling in front of the fireplace, examining the granite squares that made up the hearth.

"Okay, troops, I think these granite tiles will come up easily without breaking any of them. Bill, Sam, how about you guys take care of that while we get our digging gear."

Dr. Bonaparte looked up and noticed the two standing off to the side. "Hello, Carol, Mr. Percival. When we get the hearth up, we will be able to see what we face in terms of digging out the area under the fireplace. I suspect there will be some floorboards that will need to be removed, then the soil under that. With any luck at all, we will be able to actually dig by tomorrow. Mr. Percival, will that cause you any problems? Is there a time of day we should avoid? Will you want us out of the house while you do your prayers?"

"Thank you, Dr. Bonaparte. No problems with prayers. We are not early risers, so if you can start after nine or ten o'clock, that will be good. It will please us greatly for you to get done as quickly as possible," George Percival responded, "but, for reasons of my faith, I do need to talk to my Imam before you start digging. I will do that this afternoon. Do we know if the baby has any living relatives in Las Cruces?"

"Ami is working on that. We believe there should be some folks here, given that there is a family plot in the Masonic Cemetery. Also, the grad student's search may turn up some next of kin. Dr. Bonaparte, I have some errands to take care of. I'll check back tomorrow. Is there anything I can do or get that will help you all?" Carol inquired.

"No, I think we have everything we need. I expect the Chief of Police and the Mayor will come by. If that corresponds with your return, you can keep them out of our hair."

"Understood. Okay, I will let you all get to your tasks. Mr. Percival, I will take care of your question while I am out and about. I will see you all in a while or a while and a half."

Percival and Bonaparte chuckled at Carol's ending remark. Mr. Percival walked Carol to the front door. The two male students began working the hearth stones loose, and the rest of the crew walked out and began taking their tools out of the van.

"Dr. Montgomery," George Percival spoke as they stepped onto the porch, "I understand that Dr. Parnassus is in Morocco. May I inquire why?"

"Yes, Mr. Percival, he has returned to Marrakech. He has been asked to return to assist the Moroccan and our government with an investigation that resulted from some of the historical work he did while we were there."

"Thank you. I heard something at our Mosque about a manuscript."

"Indeed, well, the word does get around," Carol said, arching her eyebrows slightly. "I'll see you after lunch. Hello to your charming wife for me."

Carol got into her truck, and Rogue climbed onto her shoulder.

*You are skeptical about the man's question and explanation.*

### *Yes, I am. I need to let Lyle know.*

Their next stop was the coffee shop across from the University, where she and Rogue walked inside. Carol looked around as she entered and noticed Xochitl Sanchez sitting alone near the back of the café. At the counter Carol placed an order for a coffee and a bagel breakfast sandwich, with a creamer-sized cup of half-and-half for Rogue. Then, the two walked back to where Xochitl was sitting.

"May we join you?" Carol asked.

Xochitl looked up, startled, "Why yes, for sure – sit yourself down. I was just thinking about you, as it happens."

Carol sat across from Xochitl, and Rogue jumped up onto a chair between them. The barista brought Carol's coffee and Rogue's cup. "The sandwich will be ready in a few minutes," she said as she scratched between Rogue's ears.

"Great, thank you, and Rogue thanks you," Carol responded. She looked at Xochitl, who was spinning her thumbs.

Xochitl looked up with a sheepish grin. "I was wondering if you would be willing to be the best woman at my wedding?"

"Your wedding! Wow, that's great, it's also quick. Are you sure?" Carol replied.

"Yes, it seems that Lobelia and I were made for one another. I have had other partners, but never one that I was so tuned to. We both think this is the right decision."

Carol reached across the table and gave Xochitl a big abrazo. "I would be happy to be best woman for you. Who's going to give you away?" As they spoke about the planned wedding, the barista brought over Carol's sandwich.

"I have an uncle that is okay with me and my decisions. Both of my parents have passed, and no one else in the family has shown any interest or understanding. Tio has agreed to walk me down the aisle. Lobelia's mom will walk her, and Lobelia's maid of honor will be her sister."

They continued talking, until the conversation lulled as the two focused on eating. After a moment of silence, Carol swallowed the last bite of her sandwich and looked hard at Xochitl.

"Xochitl, are you aware of the dead baby thing at that house on Hadley? And the story of the man in the gray duster?"

"Dead baby, yes, the Chief has kept me up to date on the situation. Man in gray duster story, no. Does it have something to do with the dead baby? How's the family taking it?"

"It seems like it probably relates to the baby. The gray man usually shows up on cold winter nights and stands and stares at the fireplace. The daughters of the previous owners and Percival's daughter say they have seen him."

"Hmm, haunts are us, seems to be Las Cruces' by-line. You know, there are a couple of books that talk about spooks, goblins, and various haunts in New Mexico and the Las Cruces area. I may need to get them for bedtime reading."

Both women chuckled.

"Anyway, the Percivals are taking it in their stride, but the neighbors are grumbling. Seems that some of the neighbors are concerned about Muslims living there, and there is some story circulating that the Percivals are some sort of evil beings. I told Mr. Percival that I would speak to the Chief and the Mayor and see if someone could work up an article defending them and get it in the news. Lyle's grad student, who is doing some research on the house for me, has found an old diary that explains the reason for the burial. A small piece that explained that might help to ease the issues in the neighborhood. What do you think?"

"Yes, I agree. Let me talk to the boss. I think I can write the article. If he says okay, I'll notify the mayor. How's that sound? Oh, and I'll need a way to contact the grad student."

"Capital, mi amiga. Thank you. I'll text you her email, and let her know what we are doing. I'm sure she will opt to help you. Now I need to get to the office and take care of some other business."

"Okay. I'll drop by as soon as I can to show you my writing and give you a tentative date for the wedding."

"Muy bueno."

Carol stood up.  Rogue jumped down from her chair. The pair walked out of the coffee shop and headed for the truck. Xochitl remained in her chair, sighed deeply, and finished her cold coffee.

When the two returned to their office, Rogue headed for the kitchenette as Carol sat at her desk. Ami looked up and said, "You got a call from Brussels. They will call back tomorrow at about ten."

"Did they say who it was or what their call was about?"

"Interpol - wanted to ask about your sketch, I think is what they said."

"Hmm. I need to email Lyle. I'll see what he knows about Interpol calling me."

Carol opened the email on her laptop and began typing a note.

> *Lyle, I got a call from Interpol while I was out. Ami said they would call back tomorrow. Is there anything special I need to know?*
>
> *Oh, yes, I almost forgot. Mr. Percival heard something at his Mosque about a manuscript in Marrakech. The word is spreading fast among the Muslim community; it must be an important document. Be very careful, please.*
>
> *XXOO,*
>
> *Carol*

# Chapter Fourteen

*Carol, go ahead and respond to the Interpol call. We located Aliyah. She was out in the desert, visiting part of her family at a tiny oasis. Someone paid her a visit in the night in the souk, and she decided a visit to her family was in order. She also remembers a man like you sketched. I think Interpol wants to verify both your memory and your sketch. Hope you remember well. I don't know if Interpol pulled any DNA or prints from the package.*

*No more potshots, but we continue to be protected by security folks. The feared Fatwa has not emerged – yet. If we can find the thief, I understand that the Imam will burn it. I may get sent to Brussels before I get home. This is getting awfully involved – but hey, it keeps life from getting dull.*

*Luv and kisses – miss you like crazy.*

*Lyle*

Carol laid her phone on her desk and leaned back in her chair, staring at the ceiling. Rogue hopped up on her lap, kneading and purring.

Ami walked into the office and sat heavily at her desk. Carol looked over at her assistant and business partner - she looked frazzled.

"Ami, granddaughter? Not sleeping?"

"How'd you guess? We took her last night so the kids could go to a seminar or something at the university. Three o'clock in the morning – she wants to eat and play. Oh, yeah, I got a call from that developer at the old golf course on my way here. He wants another copy of your report on the Clubhouse."

"Hmm – any idea why he  wants one — and what did you do at three o'clock to get LeeAnn back to sleep?"

"Ah, yes, LeeAnn – gave her a bottle with some cereal mixed in and turned on that cute thingy-ma-jobber in her crib that goes around and around. Worked like a charm – except the monotonous dinging from the toy kept me awake for another hour. Trish is still withholding solid food, but the cereal sure worked. Don't think Trish needs to know that, though.

"Now, the developer – apparently, he is giving serious thought to moving the Clubhouse but wants to have his engineering staff review your recommendations."

"Well, we'll see what they say, I guess. I don't think the building can be moved. It's on a concrete footing, but trying to lift it will just destabilize the walls, and then—down they come. I hate to lose historic buildings like that, but I don't think this one can be moved. Clearly, the developer has no interest in renovating it and keeping it as part of his little mall or whatever he has planned for that area."

"As you say, we will see. Have you heard from Lyle?"

"Yepper. He remains alive, and the missing witch was found. He says to go ahead and talk to Interpol. Convince them that the sketch was from memory. My memory, that is," Carol said with a chuckle.

*Ah, what fools those mortal be.*

*From Shakespeare, I think. You used to read that to me when you were reading the Sunday funnies. Do they still have Sunday funnies?*

**You are right. Yes, I think they do, but we don't get the paper that used that as their comic section masthead. I will spin a convincing tale of daring do and wonder for Interpol.**

The office phone rang. Carol looked at the clock and noted that it was ten o'clock, straight up.

"Hello, this is Dr. Montgomery; how may I help you? Yes, certainly, I would be happy to speak with your Head of Criminal Investigation."

"Bonjour, Docteur Montgomery. *J'ai quelques questions. Pouvons-nous conversere en français?*" the detective asked.

"Bonjour, Monsieur. Can we converse in English, please? My French is not good," Carol responded.

"Of course, Docteur. I will ask my questions in English."

"Ah, thank you. What was your question then, sir?"

"Why did you send the package containing what turned out to be a copy of a manuscript written in Arabic to Interpol in Brussels?"

"Ah, yes, of course. The package was addressed to my husband at the University. When the package arrived there with a Brussels postmark, the department chairman was immediately concerned because there was no return address. The department chairman bagged the package and then gave it directly to me. My husband suggested that I send the package to you; he provided the address. I did not open the package because it was about the same size as the manuscript, as I recall. I was concerned, given that my husband is in Marrakech attempting to discover what became of the manuscript we found in the ruined Mosque, that it might be the missing manuscript. I understand from my husband that the Moroccan officials remain convinced that he has taken the manuscript. The U.S. Embassy people have rather the opposite viewpoint. The Embassy folks are certain that the manuscript was delivered to the Moroccan museum official, as directed."

"So, Docteur Montgomery, you thought someone might have mailed your husband the missing manuscript?"

"Yes. It could have been someone trying to show that my husband was the thief."

"Your husband said there was an old woman – a witch, I believe he called her — who helped you find the manuscript and witnessed the handover."

"Yes, there was an old woman, a seer from the Souk Semmarine, who helped us locate the manuscript. She was present when my husband handed over the manuscript. I understand that she had disappeared but has now been found. I understand that the museum official has also disappeared, I do not know if they have yet located him."

"So, Docteur, can you explain why and how you came to generate the sketch you sent to your husband and that he provided to us?"

"Of course. My husband recommended that I try to remember who else was at the handover meeting. He recalled a swarthy older man with a mustache as being present. I had a flash of recall, and from that, I generated the sketch that I sent with the manuscript."

"You drew the sketch from memory of a brief encounter with several people?"

"Yes, from my memory, sir. I am a trained Ph.D. engineer, and one of the things that I, along with most structural engineers, have learned is to pay attention to silly-seeming details and to recall those when needed. For instance, a hardly noticeable spot of rust could indicate a weakened connection in a bridge."

"I see, Docteur. I have no further questions at this time. Thank you for your time and patience."

"Thank you, Sir. Au revoir. Please do feel free to call again if there is anything else I can do to help." Carol hung up her desk phone. Ami was watching her.

"That man was worse than Inspector Clouseau. But I think I convinced him that my drawing was from memory – which it was – just not the memory he might think about."

*My witch, you were amazing. Your mind was spinning like a whirligig, but your words were precise, measured, and calm – even when you chastised him – so elegantly done. You are a Wonder Woman.*

***Okay, Brat. Your praise has penetrated my soul. A spoon of cream cheese coming up – but where can I get one of those headbands with the jewel in the middle?***

"Ami, let's go to the coffee shop. My nerves need a caffeine jitter, and her fluffiness wants a cup of cream, but I promised her a dab of cream cheese."

Their conversation was interrupted with a riff from "I Did It My Way." Carol looked at the caller ID of her phone.

"Hello, this is Carol. How may I help you, Phyllis?"

"I need to speak to you. May I come by your office?"

"I was just getting ready to go to the coffee shop. Can we talk there?"

"Yes, for sure. Which coffee shop?"

"Milagro - the one in the little shopping mall right across from the university. Do you know that one?"

"Yes. Actually, it's where I spend a fair amount of my mad money on coffee and bagels."

"Great. My assistant, Ami, and I will be there in about ten minutes. See you then."

"Got it. See you in about ten minutes."

After ordering, Carol, Ami, and Rogue found a table in a quiet corner toward the back of the coffee shop. As they sat down, Phyllis Crowne walked in, and the three watched as she searched for them. When she spotted them, she gave a small wave before ordering her coffee and joining them.

Phyllis shook hands with Ami and sat down. Rogue jumped onto her lap, purring.

"Rogue seems to like me; is she always so friendly?"

"Yes and no," Ami interjected, "she can be very picky, but she seems to know which people like cats."

*Phyllis is a good person and is soft and warm. Besides, she's Wiccan, even though she doesn't know it.*

"Ami has it nailed, Phyllis. Rogue, as with many cats, seems to know who will put up with her and who won't," Carol smiled. "Okay, what do you need to talk about?"

"Yes. Well, I think someone is following me. Ever since I started the research for that house on Hadley, I have had a feeling that I was being watched. Yesterday, I saw a vehicle that seemed to be bird-dogging me. I took some evasive moves, and the car followed."

"Hmm," Carol pondered for a moment, "I have no immediate idea who that could be or why. Have you been involved in anything else recently where someone could be stalking you?"

"Not that I know of. The feeling of being watched started a couple of days after I began visiting the Historical Research Institute."

"Let me do some checking around. Do you want me to speak to my connection at the police station?" Carol said.

"I'll ask Iggy if he has heard anything," Ami offered.

"Iggy?" Phyllis queried.

"My husband. He's with the State Police." Ami replied.

"Thank you both, but I don't have any sense of danger, so let's let it ride. I wanted to let you know because I heard that you and Dr. Parnassus had been followed before he returned to Morocco. I thought there might be some connection."

"Very perceptive, Phyllis. Have you always had these feelings or senses of stuff?" Carol asked.

"Actually, yes. Let me give you my brief history — it may help you understand where I'm coming from. For starters, I am 'mixed-race'. My mother was the result of a liaison between an Aboriginal woman and a British man. My grandmother was one of the 'stolen children' and was trained to be a housekeeper. My mother, in her turn, was educated at a mission school for mixed-race children and married a Brit.

Our family is a member of the Wurundjeri People. Our ancestors were on the site of Melbourne long before any white person came to Australia. We remain the traditional custodians of the land. I have an uncle who is a respected cleverman."

"Wait a minute, a cleverman? What is that?" Carol asked.

"A witch doctor in the parlance of the whites. A traditional healer. He is said to be able to read people's ailments over the phone."

"Okay, I see," Carol nodded in thought, "Go on, please — your story is fascinating."

"Well, the stories in the family say that all of the women, my gram and mum included, have special abilities to sense what you might call vibrations. I think I might have the same ability. It is very handy, sometimes — like when researching the files at the Historical Research Institute and the courthouse. My sense sort of directed me to the right places to look."

"Now that is interesting," Ami said, "No wonder you were able to find that old diary and will."

"Yes. And for that same reason, I am not concerned about whoever is following me. The vibrations I am sensing are not bad; they seem to be mostly curiosity."

"Okay, I will go with your sense, Phyllis, but if anything changes, please let me know — immediately," Carol stated.

"Thank you, Dr. Montgomery. By the way, do you have any idea when Dr. Parnassus will be back from Morocco? I want to confirm the use of this research for my thesis. There is a really interesting story in what I have found so far, and it allows a peek in some depth into the history of the time."

"No, not really. Dr. Parnassus recently emailed me that he is okay and may need to go to Brussels, but other than that — no return date yet. I believe he will say yes to your thesis. I will mention your query when I text him."

"Again, thank you."

A familiar riff began to play, and Carol quickly took the phone from her pocket. "Hello, Mr. Percival; how may I help you? ...Yes, certainly. I was due to head your way as soon as I finished my conversation with another client. Okay, good. I'll see you shortly."

"I take it Mr. Percival has an emergency," Ami remarked.

"Yes, the archaeologists have begun to dig, and he is worried about how they will handle whatever they find. We need to drive by his house."

"Dr. Montgomery, may I join you there? I have done all of this research, but I have not seen the house," Phyllis asked.

"But of course, Phyllis. Let's finish our coffee — Rogue has eaten all of her cream cheese — and we'll see you there."

Carol pulled up and stopped in front of Mr. Percival's house, with Phyllis pulling up right behind her. The University van was there, its rear doors standing open. George Percival was standing on the front porch and walked out to the sidewalk as Carol exited her truck, with Phyllis not far behind her. Mr. Percival's eyes widened slightly when they looked past Carol.

"Dr. Montgomery, glad you could come."

"Mr. Percival, my pleasure. You remember my assistant, Ami, and this is the young woman who is doing the historical research on your house, Phyllis Crowne."

"Of course - Ms. Lopez, Miss Crowne," George Percival nodded to them.

Percival walked into the house, followed by the three women. Rogue remained in the truck. Phyllis gave Carol an eyebrow rise and followed.

*Boss, that man is sweating like a pig. It all started when he saw Phyllis get out of her truck.*

**Thank you, Rogue. I also sense that he is nervous. Strange. Phyllis gave me a look. We'll have to see what transpires.**

The lead archaeologist, Dr. Alice Bonaparte, kneeling by the fireplace, stood as the four entered the dining room, "Carol, nice to see you. The Mayor and Chief of Police came by yesterday just as we were leaving. I gave them a quick look and explanation, and they left, apparently happy."

"Alice, this is Phyllis Crowe, my husband's grad student, researching the house and the ownership chain - and here is my assistant, Ami Lopez."

"A pleasure to meet you, Ami and Miss Crowne. May I call you Phyllis – I tend not to lean on formalities."

"Yes, that would be fine, Dr. Bonaparte," Phyllis replied.

"Please, Alice – that informality should work both ways. Carol, the dig is going well. Nothing to report yet, but we are only down about a foot."

"Dr. Montgomery, Dr. Bonaparte, that is why I need to speak with you." George Percival began. "In my faith, Islam, exhumation and reburial are Haram — forbidden — unless absolutely necessary. I understand that, in this case, the exhumation and reburial are necessary, but may I ask my Imam to watch over the process? I must admit, it makes me extremely nervous, and his opinion and blessing—as it were—would make me feel better."

"Dr. Bonaparte, what do you say?" Carol asked, looking at the archaeologist.

"Carol, Mr. Percival, I have no problem with the Imam observing our work. I only ask that he stay back and not offer advice. Many people will do just that, and I believe that we are competent to do what is necessary."

George asked, "Dr. Bonaparte, what will you do with the remains if and when you find them?"

"Good question, Mr. Percival. If, as I anticipate, we find only skeletal remains, we will bag them in an opaque plastic bag for delivery to a mortuary for subsequent contact with living relatives and reburial. I understand that there is an appropriate family plot at the Masonic Cemetery. If there is anything more, we may need to acquire a body bag, but I doubt that will be the case."

"Thank you, Dr. Bonaparte. I am much relieved. I will call my Imam and let him know that he may observe."

"Dr. Montgomery, we need to talk after we leave," Phyllis muttered to Carol.

Carol looked at Phyllis, who had a very concerned look on her face, and replied, "For sure, Phyllis - and please just call me Carol."

"Mr. Percival, Alice - it sounds like things are as under control as they can be. Ami and I have a report to finish for the city, and I need to chat with Phyllis. So, if you will excuse us, we need to leave."

"Have fun, Carol. I detest reports, but I'll be doing one myself for this exercise," Alice Bonaparte said as she knelt down beside the small pit in the fireplace.

"I'll see you to the door, and thank you again for coming by on such short notice," George Percival said as he walked toward the front door.

"My pleasure, Mr. Percival—that is what you are paying me for."

Carol, Ami, and Phyllis walked out to their vehicles. Ami climbed into Carol's truck, and Carol walked back to Phyllis's car.

"Okay, Phyllis, what do you need to tell me? Whatever it is has you just a bit stirred up, if I can read faces at all."

"Yes. First, Mr. Percival is one of the people that have been following me. However, I think I know why now. As a Muslim, an exhumation in his house is extremely upsetting. I have some Muslim friends at NMSU and back home, and I understand his concerns. Secondly, I have just put together, in my mind, some of the diary. There are some pages that I have not yet found, but I believe that, based on what I have, they will not find bones. I think the original owner exhumed and cremated the baby, then reburied the urn under the fireplace."

"Okay, why would that be a problem? Reburying an urn is actually a bit easier than dealing with a skeleton."

"Normally, it would make no difference. However, cremation is Haram for Muslims. I fear that finding an urn will really upset both the Imam and Mr. Percival."

"Ah, yes, I see. Let me email Alice and give her a heads-up. I'll ask her to try to make the discovery of an urn rather than bones, if that is what they find, as slick and simple as possible. I doubt the Imam will miss that, but perhaps Alice can minimize any distress."

"Good, I don't know what else you can do. However, I know the archaeologist will find an urn. The vibrations I get from the pit confirm that."

"Thank you, Phyllis. Come by the office why don't you, and we'll consume a cuppa or some more coffee."

"Thank you, Carol. I would be pleased to have a cuppa. Do you have any Darjeeling?"

"I believe I do."

# Chapter Fifteen

The government jet made a smooth landing at the Brussels Airport and taxied to the Blue Corner terminal. A small fleet of cars was parked nearby. Bill Spencer, Lyle Parnassus, and the security team exited the aircraft and walked to the parked cars. An officious man in a suit greeted them and directed them to a limousine.

"Bill, I take it that guy is our Interpol liaison," Lyle said as the security team closed the vehicle's doors.

"Yes, that is the Head of Criminal Investigation in the Brussels office of Interpol. He is nearly as important as he thinks he is," Bill replied. "We will want to be very polite to him. I think he may be the person who interviewed Carol over the phone."

"Okay, I will be at my most polite. I gather the guy speaks English. My French is absolutely stinko. I struggle to read papers written in French – even with my handy dandy French dictionary at my right hand."

"I think he does. He'll likely start off in French – they are renowned for that – but he will switch readily to English, I believe."

"Okay, that sounds fine. I take it we are headed to Interpol's Brussels complex."

"That's the goal. My understanding is that Interpol wants you to look at a picture of the guy that they are surveilling and tell them if he was the guy you saw at the handover. After their sting and his arrest, they want you to ID him in a line-up. He won't be able to see you at any time."

"Ah, yes, the perks of being a temporary spook, I guess."

Bill laughed and settled back in the seat of the limo. "Yep, there are perks."

"Will Interpol get the manuscript as part of the sting? Or is this just another step in the process? I really would like to go home, and my students and the department chair are probably wondering if I'll ever be back. And I miss Carol more than I would have thought possible."

"Lyle, my understanding is that the sting is designed to recover the manuscript and bag the thief. It seems he is known to Interpol. They have a large dossier on him but have not been able to bust him before this. He's been sort of a Pink Panther-type guy. If their sting goes according to plan, several police departments in about a dozen countries will be happy as clams, not to mention our skeptical friends in Morocco."

"Yeah, it would be good to get the manuscript back to its home and have that Imam burn his Fatwa. Has anyone found the Moroccan official that was involved?"

"No, not yet, but my sources think he may be by-catch from the sting."

"That would be good. I take it the old witch is okay and said yes to the sketch?"

"Yes, she and her rangy black cat are back in their slot in the souk. She does command some respect among the Moroccan folks, so she will be fine."

"Bill, Carol asked me to ask if Interpol has done a DNA analysis of the package she sent."

"My understanding is they have done so. That is part of why they think the Moroccan guy may be by-catch. May I ask why Carol was curious?"

"She is extremely observant, as you might expect from an engineer. She said there were some smudges on the package, and an odor of tobacco. So, she thought those might point to whoever had handled the package or the manuscript copy."

"Interesting. I think that Interpol might have gotten a lead using DNA analysis that pointed them at the principal bad guy."

"A woman's intuition. Never fails, does it?"

Bill Spencer chuckled and held the door into the building for Lyle.

The group soon exited the old office building in Brussels. Three men in handcuffs were being escorted by uniformed officers in the lead, followed by Bill Spencer, the Chief of Interpol Investigations, and Lyle Parnassus, who carried a small briefcase.

As the handcuffed men reached the police van, a stranger came running along the sidewalk, screaming in Arabic. The screaming man snatched the briefcase from Lyle and continued running. A fusillade of shots rang from the roof of a building across the street. Bill roughly grabbed Lyle in reaction and threw him to the ground.

The uniformed officers tried to shove the handcuffed men into the van. An officer with the three men spun and fell to the street as more shots rang out. The assailant that had tried to make off with the briefcase stumbled and fell to the ground. As one of the security guards started toward him, he exploded. Bits of the man, blood, and shards of parchment flew across the street and the sidewalk.

The shots ceased.

Any remaining Interpol officers sprinted toward the building across the street. Bill Spencer lay on top of Lyle, very still. The four men, three prisoners and the officer closest to them, lay in pools of blood by the van. One of them moving weakly and crying out. A member of security was down and bleeding, the other tending to his wounds.

# Chapter Sixteen

Dr. Alice Bonaparte, the archaeologist, scratched her head and looked at the item her team had just exposed in the fireplace. Her cell phone played a jazzy riff. "Hello, this is Dr. Bonaparte. How may I help you? Oh, hello Carol. What's up?"

"Alice, I just had a conversation with Phyllis Crowe regarding the diary she found at the Historical Research Institute. She said that although some pages were missing, she is certain that you will not find bones but an urn of ashes."

"Hmm - that's interesting. We just exposed a metal box. No bones or urns yet. I think we probably need to report the box to the city and let them open it. What do you think?"

"Probably, yes, but let me come by and look. Is it still in the ground?"

"Yes. What should I tell Mr. Percival? According to the law, as I understand it, the contents of the box are his since he's the property owner."

"If he asks, tell him we will have the box inspected, and since he owns the property, the contents will be his to do with as he wishes. Try to avoid telling him about the potential urn. Cremation is also Haram to Muslims. Is the Imam there?"

"Not yet. I understand from Mr. Percival that he got delayed and will be here later."

"Hmm – Okay, try not to make the urn, if that is what's under the box, an issue if you can."

"Okey dokey, smokey. See you in a while. I think it's coffee break time. I'll leave the box as it is and call the mayor's office."

⌂ ⌂ ⌂

"Damn, Alice, that looks like an old document box. Did the mayor say anything about sending someone, or should we open it?"

"The mayor suggested taking it to the Historical Research people or to the special collections department at NMSU. I guess we can open it and see if it has anything of immediate value versus historical value."

George Percival walked up behind the two women with a tall man in a robe and cap.

"Hello, Dr. Montgomery and Dr. Bonaparte," Mr. Percival said, "what do you have there?"

"Oh, hello, Mr. Percival," Carol responded as she stood up and turned around. "This is a metal box that appears to be right above the remains that Dr. Bonaparte is digging for. Is this your Imam?"

"Yes, this is Imam Ahmed. Imam Ahmed, this is Dr. Montgomery, the engineer, and Dr. Bonaparte, the archaeologist that I have been telling you about."

"I am pleased to meet you," the Imam said. "So, what is in the box? Do you know? Could it be the remains of the child?"

"We don't know yet. We have to lift the box carefully and then open it," Alice Bonaparte replied. "We have notified the city about finding it. The mayor suggested we give it to the university or to the Historical Research Institute. Technically, Mr. Percival, since the box is on your private property, the box and whatever is in it is yours."

"Hmm. Well, if it is human remains, I, of course, do not want them but wish them to be re-interred in a cemetery. If the box contains something else, then I would have to decide about whatever it is," George Percival responded. "So, go ahead and lift it as you need to, and then we can find the answer."

The Imam shook his head in the affirmative. Alice Bonaparte returned to her kneeling position and began to clear the soil from on and around the box. After about ten minutes of careful work with a trowel, spade, and brush, Alice lifted the box from the hole and set it on the tarp next to her. As she lifted the box, she noticed a small, round object that appeared to be a lid. It was quickly covered by the soil that tumbled back into the hole. Alice gave Carol a quick glance.

Carol had seen the object as well and gave Alice an affirmative eyebrow rise. The two men were focused on the box, while the students who stood behind Alice and Carol watched with rapt attention.

Alice attempted to open the box lid, but it was locked. A very simple keyed lock that was full of dirt could be seen. The archeologist looked back at her student helpers and asked, "Can one of you hand me my digging kit, please?"

One of the young men handed Alice a small toolbox. She rummaged around inside for a moment, then took out a small pick-like tool. Using the tool, Alice cleaned the dirt from the lock. Then, she took a small, flat tool from her kit. Alice inserted the tool in the lock, jiggled it about for a moment, then turned it and opened the box lid.

"The well-prepared archaeologist always has the appropriate tool," Dr. Bonaparte spoke proudly, looking at her students and the two men. "And a knowledge of lock picking also helps."

Everyone peered intently into the small metal box. On top of whatever else was in the box were a baby's cradle cap and a frilly dress. The clothes were carefully lifted out of the box and placed into a plastic bag that one of the students handed the archaeologist. Under the clothes were a small stack of documents that appeared to be hand-written pages. Alice carefully removed the documents, which were brown and brittle, and placed them in another bag.

"We should get some acid-free page protectors for these," Alice said as she carefully placed the bag of pages next to the bag of clothes.

There was nothing under the documents. The bottom of the box was surprisingly intact but had some rust holes in it.

"Dr. Bonaparte, I am immensely curious about what is written on those pages," Mr. Percival remarked, "but I believe they should be given to the Historical Research Institute to go along with the material that Miss Crowne found there. Perhaps she can copy them and provide me with the copies."

"Mr. Percival, I agree with you," Alice Bonaparte said. "Carol, can you contact Phyllis Crowne and let her know? I will have one of the students run to Staples and get some covers and a folder to hold them."

Carol nodded in the affirmative, stood up from her squatting position, and stepped out the front door. Alice gave one of the students her credit card and asked them to drive to Staples and get a package of protective plastic covers. Mr. Percival and the Imam stood back out of the way and looked at one another.

"Dr. Bonaparte," the Imam asked, "are you going to continue to dig for the remains now, or should we wait to find out what the papers say? It seems to me they may have some important bearing on what lies beneath the box."

"Imam Ahmed, I believe that we should perhaps call it a day. Finding the box and its contents is actually an important part of this excavation. Whatever lies below the box is not going to go anywhere – after all, it has been here for about 100 years.

Another twenty-four hours will make no difference. That is if Mr. Percival is willing to put up with us for another day or so."

"Imam Ahmed, Dr. Bonaparte, I agree that another day will not change anything. I would like to have my dining room back, and I also dearly want to get the rest of the project completed and my home stabilized. However, dealing with the remains is even more important in the eyes of Allah, and for me and my family's peace of mind. Please begin again tomorrow and complete your work."

"Thank you, Mr. Percival. The extra time will not cost you anything more than the inconvenience. I am sure it will allow us to do the best possible job of dealing with and re-interring the remains."

# Chapter Seventeen

Carol clicked on the email from her husband that had come in while she was at George Percival's home. She had alerted Phyllis Crowe, who had connected with Alice Bonaparte and obtained the metal box and its contents.

Now, she read the first email she had gotten from her husband in four days.

*Carol, My Luv —*

*Sorry to be so slow with emails. Probably a good reason for this delay, though. We were shot up and bombed in Brussels. Bill Spencer is dead — which is why I am alive and well. But let me explain.*

*We got together with Interpol in Brussels, and they sprung their trap on the manuscript thieves. We recovered the manuscript in what appeared to be good condition. The Brussels police arrested the thieves — the Moroccan gov't guy, a Middle Eastern artifact peddler, and the dealer that we saw in Marrakech. Indeed, as your intuition had predicted,*

*Interpol found DNA evidence as well as some smudged fingerprints on the envelope that was mailed to me.*

*We were leaving the place where they did the sting. I had the manuscript in a briefcase. The police were loading the perps into their van, and Bill and I were about to get into our limo when a man came running and screaming along the sidewalk. The man snatched the briefcase from me and ran on. Gunfire erupted from a building across the street. Bill pushed me down and fell on top of me. One of the cops and the prisoners were felled by the gunfire. The running guy was shot, fell to the sidewalk, and exploded.*

*Bill was pronounced dead at the scene. I was bruised by the fall and covered with Bill's blood but otherwise uninjured. There were pieces of the runner scattered around, along with fragments of the manuscript. The perps were all dead, as was the Brussels policeman. One of the Interpol guys and one of our security guys were wounded but are fixed and okay.*

*I spent a day in hospital and then a day dealing with Interpol and the Moroccan government. The Moroccans agreed to accept the copy of the manuscript in lieu of the real thing. Interpol will send them such fragments of the original as they can find. The Imam in Marrakech has agreed to burn the Fatwa, so I will not need to be looking over my shoulder all the time.*

*It seems that the shooting and explosion were the result of the centuries-old feud between the Sunni and the Shia. The manuscript was thought to have been written or dictated by Mohammed, so both sects claimed it. The guy who blew himself up was apparently a Sunni, and the shooters were Shia. If we can't have it, no one can.*

*I should be home in a day or two. I have to deliver the copy to Rabat, then they will bring me and Bill's remains home. I understand that he will be buried in Arlington National Cemetery. I may be asked to stay for the funeral – we'll see.*

*Okay, my luv. Missing you more than you can know. Take care.*

*Lyle*

Carol leaned back in her chair and signed deeply. Ami looked over at her with a quizzical expression.

"Lyle was damn-near murdered in Brussels. He's okay, but I get the sense he is struggling with what happened. His friend Bill Spencer was killed, and a guy blew himself to bits – all because of an old parchment manuscript. He should be home in a few days."

*Boss, are you going to be okay? Your brain is whirling like I've never seen it before.*

***Rogue, I don't know. But I need to respond to Lyle's email.***

"Ami, I'm going to the house; get myself a large glass of nerve potion and send Lyle a response. If anyone except Phyllis calls, tell them I'm indisposed. If it is Phyllis, have her call me on my cell."

"Got it, Carol. Be good to yourself. What happened to Lyle is not your doing. Don't punish yourself."

*Lyle,*

*Oh shit, oh dear. You have no idea – actually, you probably do – how your email has torn me up. But – a good thing – you are well and in one piece, if not happy. Don't hesitate to stay for the funeral if that is what feels right for you. I take it Bill has family in that area.*

*But, let me bend your ear with what's going on here – which, interestingly enough, has a Muslim involved. Phyllis found a will and a diary for the original owner of the house. The diary indicated that they had re-buried their dead child under the fireplace in the dining room. The city brought in Dr. Bonaparte from NMSU to dig the fireplace. Plan to re-inter the remains in the family plot in the Masonic Cemetery. Phyllis thinks they may have cremated the bones and re-buried the urn. Mr. Percival has his Imam observing. Dr. Bonaparte found a metal box, and it appeared that an urn was just below the box. The box contained some baby clothes and several hand-written pages, which Phyllis has. She has not yet reported what they say. Phyllis would like to use the material she has gathered for her thesis.*

*A bit of a ramble of events. Otherwise, everything goes on as usual.*

*Miss you more than you can know. Take care and try not to get shot at again, my luv.*

*Carol*

The email was quickly written and sent. Carol leaned back on the couch, took a sip of her wine, then closed her eyes and tried to blank her mind. Rogue jumped onto her lap and began to knead.

*Boss, your head is still spinning. Think about the beach and the ocean lapping on the sand. I've heard that helps.*

***Thank you, my familiar and friend. The world is going by way too fast. I wonder if Lyle and I can arrange to get a Blessing Way Ceremony in Dinetah. I need to ask him to contact Margaret and Bidzii Tsosie when he responds to my email.***

The melody of "I Did It My Way" interrupted her spiraling thoughts.

"Hello, Phyllis. Thank you for calling. I just exchanged emails with Dr. Parnassus, and I mentioned to him your interest in using the Percival house stuff for your thesis. No, I haven't heard back from him yet. I think he is in the air somewhere between Brussels and Rabat. That's great, what do they say? Okay, yes, come on by. I have some Malbec I would be happy to share. Okay, see you in a few."

Carol clicked off her phone and leaned back again. The doorbell chiming jerked her awake from the brief snooze she had fallen into. She opened the front door, greeted by Phyllis Crowne standing there with a sheaf of papers in her hand.

"Phyllis, come in. I had dozed off. Too much stress, I guess. Park yourself on the couch, and let me get you a glass of wine."

"Thank you, Dr. Montgomery. I think I'll take a pass on the wine. I have to drive to Alamogordo in a while to hook up with an old friend. Here're copies of the stuff from the box. An interesting read. A long note from a distraught father and an explanation for why the urn and the box are under the fireplace. Thank you for letting Dr. Parnassus know about my thoughts. I hope he is well and will be home before too long. Now, I need to run. My roomie is waiting in the car."

"Thank you, Phyllis. Have a safe drive. Let me know when you get back. We'll have to try for the wine another time. Oh, and again, please call me Carol."

"Alright, Carol. You take care also. I should be back the day after tomorrow. I'll let myself out, you continue your kicking-back." With that, Phyllis walked out and closed the door.

Carol sat back on the couch and indulged in another sip of her wine as she began to read the sheaf of papers. She was about halfway through the documents when the doorbell chimed. Standing outside the door, when she opened it, were Xochitl and Lobelia with a bag of food and another bottle of wine.

# Chapter Eighteen

Dr. Alice Bonaparte knelt in front of the fireplace with her student diggers around her.

"Okay, folks, here we go," Dr. Bonaparte said, "the first thing is always to carefully remove any loose soil and probe gently to determine if the object is hard or soft and how deep it is beneath the surface."

The students all mumbled quietly and watched as Dr. Bonaparte slowly and methodically removed the loose soil from the top of the object. The Imam stood behind the group, saying nothing. As she brushed and scooped, the object was slowly revealed to be the top of a larger vessel. Both appeared to be high-quality porcelain, and there was a design on the top of what was apparently a lid on an urn-shaped container. The Imam grumbled to himself and stood back from the group. After about a half hour of brushing, careful digging, and gentle scooping, the object revealed itself to be a crematory urn. Mr. Percival, watching next to the Imam, groaned. The Imam began mumbling a prayer. One of the students reached into the hole, carefully lifted the urn out, and set it on the tarp next to Dr. Bonaparte.

"Well folks, I believe that we have found the remains of the child that was interred here. The urn is consistent with a period in the early 20th Century, probably 1910 to 1912. That agrees with the diary that Miss Crowe found and with the contents of the document in the box. We need to carefully wrap the urn and box it. I have made an arrangement with one of the funeral parlors in town to take charge of it and to see it re-interred in the family's plot in the Masonic Cemetery."

Another of the students went out to the team's van and came back with a strong cardboard box and a length of bubble wrap. Mr. Percival sat on the couch in the living room with his head in his hands, and the Imam sat next to him, praying. The digging team carefully wrapped the urn in bubble wrap and placed it in the box, taping the box closed. As the group stood up, there was a knock at the front door. A well-dressed man entered the dining room and showed his card to Dr. Bonaparte.

"Folks, this is the gentleman from the funeral home. He will take the urn and will give us a receipt, which I will provide to the city, and a copy to Mr. Percival if he wants it," Dr. Bonaparte stated.

The funeral director handed Dr. Bonaparte a document, and she gave him the box. He thanked her, spoke some parting words to Mr. Percival and the Imam, and left. The archeologist and her team refilled the hole, picked up their tarp and tools, and loaded the van. Dr. Bonaparte stepped into the living room and sat in the overstuffed chair across from the couch.

"Imam Ahmed, Mr. Percival, we have removed and arranged for the re-interment of the urn. I understand your upset and that the presence of a cremated body has, to some extent, defiled your home. However, the urn is now gone, so I trust that you will be able to ameliorate the defilement. The folks who were doing the stabilization of the house and fireplace will now be able to finish their work. I want to thank you for your patience and for your understanding. If you wish, Mr. Percival, I will provide you a copy of the receipt for the transfer of the urn."

"Dr. Bonaparte, we thank you for your work," the Imam said. "According to my understanding of the Quran, Allah will make the dead person whole again in the afterlife. Since the cremation was done long ago, and before the Percivals owned the home, Allah will not look unkindly on them. They will continue as they have, and the house will be as it was. Their upset over the presence of a cremated person will diminish."

"Thank you, Imam Ahmed. My team and I will leave now. I wish you the very best, Mr. Percival."

"Thank you, Dr. Bonaparte," Mr. Percival said. "If you contact Dr. Montgomery, will you please give her my regards and ask her to stop by before the stabilization crew gets started again?"

"I will certainly do that, Mr. Percival," Dr. Bonaparte replied and walked out to the van. The students finished loading the van, climbed in, and they departed.

⌂ ⌂ ⌂

"Hi, Carol, Alice Bonaparte here. We are done. The urn is with the funeral folks. Mr. Percival is understandably distraught. He asked if you would stop by and see him before the stabilization crew gets started again."

"Thank you, Alice. Yes, I plan on going by tomorrow in the morning."

"Great. What do you hear from Lyle? I heard that the History Department is getting antsy and wants him back."

"Lyle should be home in a very few days. He may need to spend a day or two in Arlington to attend the funeral of the guy who went with him to Morocco. Other than being rightfully unwound, he is fine and is looking forward to the boredom of being a history prof."

"Understood. Take care of yourself. Let's get together for a quiet coffee, tea, or something alcoholic one of these first days."

"Alice, I will let you know when I have a quiet afternoon if there is such a thing anymore, and we can sit and chew the fat over something liquid."

"For sure. Give me a ring-a-ding. Okay, Cheers for now. I've gotta get these kids home and do the same for myself."

Late that night, a man in a gray duster and hat stood before the empty fireplace. He stood there for about a half hour, then turned to the west and disappeared through the wall.

⌂ ⌂ ⌂

"Carol, I'm just leaving Dulles. I should be in El Paso by about six this afternoon. Looking forward to seeing you and hugging you at the gate. Got to shut off the phone now."

"I'll be there with bells on. Rogue says she has missed you despite referring to you as the ogre. I have more than missed you. Have a safe flight. Love you."

"Okay, they just announced our immediate departure. Love you too, dear."

When the time came, Carol was pacing back and forth in front of the arrival gate. The woman at the counter watched her, then walked around the counter and spoke to Carol. "Ma'am, is there anything I can do? You seem to be agitated."

"Oh, thank you, no. I'm waiting for my husband to get here on the flight from Dulles. I haven't seen him for nearly a month. He's been in Morocco and Europe, and I have seriously missed him."

"Okay, I understand. My husband is military, and I fret and worry every time he is gone. Can I get you a cup of tea or a bottle of water?"

"No, thank you. I'll just wear a groove in the floor here. The flight is on time, right?"

"Yes, ma'am, it is. Are you sure you wouldn't like to sit down?"

"Naw, I'd just squirm a hole in the seat. Besides, I need the exercise."

"Okay. Oh, hey, they just announced the arrival of your flight. Shouldn't be more than five or ten minutes."

"Thank you. Now I think I'll just go and stare out the window. Maybe watching the plane taxi in will calm me – hah – yeh – for sure."

The woman laughed and returned to her work, getting ready for the arrival and loading for the next flight. Carol walked to the window that looked out at the loading ramp and watched the big jet taxi in and the ramp roll out and connect. The first of the passengers emerged from the ramp into the arrival area. Lyle walked out, looking slightly bedraggled. Carol was standing in the area just outside the arrival ramp. They saw one another simultaneously. Lyle rushed toward Carol, and they embraced tightly as people walked around them, a few shaking their heads, a few others smiling broadly.

"Oh, my god, my love. I feared that I might never see you again," Carol said, tears streaming from her eyes.

"Ditto, my dear. You cannot imagine how happy I am to be back and to hold you."

"Let's get your luggage and get home. You look like you've been shot at and missed and shit at and hit."

"Yes. Your words have the ring of reality, and it's scary."

Arms around one another, Carol and Lyle walked toward the stairs and the baggage claim area.

⌂ ⌂ ⌂

"Xochitl, Lobelia, I'm so pleased for you," Lyle said, offering his coffee cup in a toast.

"Thank you, Lyle. We are excited and looking forward to having you at the wedding and having Carol as my best woman," Xochitl responded.

Lobelia nodded in the affirmative and gave Xochitl a quick kiss on her ear. Phyllis Crowe stood up, stretched, and hugged the two other women, one with each arm.

"Carol, Lyle, Xochitl, Lobelia. I have a class I have to get to. I'll leave you all to finish enjoying Lyle's delightful breakfast and Carol's coffee. Dr. Parnassus, I will see you tomorrow at ten to discuss my thesis, right?"

"That's right, Phyllis. I take it you have an outline worked up, and I know you have most of your research materials in hand," Lyle responded.

"You'll be at the wedding, I hope," Lobelia said.

"You couldn't keep me away," Phyllis responded and headed toward the front door. She stopped, looked back at Carol, and waved her index finger in a wand-like motion, "Carol, thank you for everything to date. It is really nice to know… a cleverwoman with a clevercat."

Carol nodded, grinned, and winked, "Thank you, my young friend." Rogue meowed and sneezed.

*She knows!*

**Yes. I think she has all along.**

"Let me walk with you, please," Lyle said, standing and walking with Phyllis. "I want to say a couple of words between Prof and acolyte."

Carol sat and smiled. Xochitl looked at her, grinned, and said, "It is so very nice to have one's mate home and safe."

Lyle walked back into the kitchen and sat down. "Okay, my dear, I heard you on the phone to Mr. Percival this morning. What's up?"

"Nothing serious. Mr. Percival was just letting me know that the stabilizing crew had finished and that he would be sending me a check as soon as Ami can get him a final invoice. He did say that his daughter had told him about the gray man but had not seen the gray man again since the re-interment, and he hoped the specter was now gone permanently. He and his family seem to have recovered from the crematory urn being in their home. By the by, Ami was unable to locate any living relatives in our area. There appears to be a cousin in Florida and another in Dallas, neither of which expressed any interest in the situation. On the strength of the will, the Masonic Cemetery was able to approve the reinterment of the ashes in the family plot. The baby girl now lies at her parents' feet."

"That's good. You were going to tell us what was in the document that was in the box."

"Ah, yes. Interesting story, that."

"Well, don't keep us on tenterhooks," Xochitl said. "I need to finish my report about the situation for the Chief and the Mayor."

"It seems that a very young couple were squatting on what they hoped would become their home place. They were expecting a baby. The house they were in was a very simple adobe, but they had no water, no outhouse yet, and no way to heat the home."

"That sounds like a very typical situation for that time," Lyle said.

"Yes. The baby was born during a rare winter snowstorm and died only a couple of weeks later. The young couple were planning a trip north to Santa Fe in search of a better situation, and the child passed on the night they were supposed to leave. They wrapped the body in whatever baby clothes they had and placed the child in a relatively shallow grave close to their house. Grieving, they headed for Santa Fe.

"According to the diary Phyllis found and the document in the box, the young man was successful in Santa Fe and became an attorney. He made a bundle of money handling land adjudication cases. The couple had three more children, all of whom were healthy and robust. When their oldest boy was about eighteen, they decided to return to Las Cruces and try again. They packed up their family and took the newly established train south. When they got to Cruces, the man, no longer quite so young, established a practice and got into the real estate business on the side. He was able to acquire a parcel in a new subdivision at the place where their child was buried.

"Long story short – they exhumed the remains of their child, had the bones cremated, and buried them under the fireplace in their new home."

"Hmm, so why the fireplace?" Lobelia asked.

"The child died because of the cold. They wanted to provide her a warm place for eternity – hence the fireplace."

"And the box of clothes on the document?" Xochitl asked.

"A bonnet and dress that the child might have worn, and the story of why she was there."

"How about the man in the gray duster and hat?" Lyle asked. "Was that the grieving father, perhaps?"

"Lyle, I think yes. Apparently, despite his success as an attorney and being the father of a family, the man never quite got over grieving for that first child. If there is a specter, that would be why."

"So," Lobelia offered, "with the remains in the ground near the man and his wife, the specter can move on."

"Yes, Lobelia, I think that would follow," Carol said. "Now, folks, I have to get to work. I have a request to look at an old adobe across from the cathedral in Doña Ana. It sounds like a juicy contract in the offing."

"I have beau coups catching up to do and a class to prep," Lyle said, "so I'd best get my derriere in gear, too."

"Okay, folks. Thank you for breakfast and a nice quiet time," Xochitl responded. "Lobelia and I need to sit down and do some more planning; then I have a report to write for the Chief."

The two women got up and left. Carol sat for a few more minutes, just looking at Lyle.

"Dear heart, what say we talk to the Tsosies about a Blessing Way Ceremony? I think we need something to flush the negative crap we've been dealing with?"

"I had a similar thought. I'll get in touch with Bidzii when I get to my office."

The local newspaper had a brief article on page five about a walker who was going by the Masonic Cemetery just after dark.

The person looked over the wall and noticed a freshly turned and re-sodded spot in front of a tombstone. Standing next to the newly sodded area was a man in a gray duster and gray hat. He seemed to be speaking to the new sod.

The walker looked away, and when they looked back, the man in the gray duster had vanished.

*Acknowledgements*

*As always, I owe my wife a big hug, and thank you for reading and reviewing this book. Her suggestions made it a better story. I need to express my appreciation for the hard work and timely editing that my publisher provided. Thank you, Tiffany, Senka, and Miri, as well as all the other persons who contributed to the editing and publication.*

# About Fenton R. Kay

Fenton is a retired biologist whose writing includes eight prior novels, twenty-two publications in the scientific literature, and several poems published in the Las Vegas Review-Journal and online at Eskimo Pie.

Fenton lives with his wife, two grandsons, four dogs, five aquaria, a red-eared slider turtle with his own pond, and eight cats. He enjoys watching Nature and NOVA on PBS and sitting under the gazebo in his backyard, watching the birds, butterflies, moths, and bees on the flowers.

"The Man in the Gray Duster" is the fourth installment of Fenton's Carol Montgomery Mystery series and the first to be published with Las Cruces based company Borderlands Media.

You can find Fenton online at:

kaylibros.casa

Facebook.com/KayratSpeaks/

Goodreads.com/author/show/19071122.Fenton_R_Kay

# Other Books by Fenton R. Kay

**The O'Flaithearta Biological Consultants Mysteries**
    #1 - Le Cochon Volant: The Flying Pig
    #2 - Bear Market
    #3 - Eye of Newt, Skin of Toad
    #4 - Of Rats and Drones

**Carol Montgomery Mysteries**
    #1 - The Old Courthouse
    #2 - A Piano in the Night
    #3 - La Llorona

**Young Adult and Middle Reader Novels**
    Chipmunk Jumped Over Him
    The Jaguar Drum

**Children's Books**
    Dear Jennifer: The Jenny Princess Letters

**Writings on Art and Poetry**
    Still Life Musings: A Small Haiga Collection